The Guinea Pigs of
Brierley Bramble

The Guinea Pigs of Brierley Bramble

J.P. Stringer

A tale of Nature and Magic
for children and adults

Brierley Bramble UK

Text copyright © J.P. Stringer 2020

Illustrations copyright © Kim Fowler 2020

Cover design & illustration by
Adrian Doan Kim 2020. © J.P. Stringer

Formatting & layout by Fiona Birney

ISBN. 978-1-8381321-1-8

For
Jean & Al

With love

The Stringers, Patersons
& Howarths too

*The Universe works
in ways we cannot see...*

Contents

Chapter 1

A Very Strange Night

IT was almost a white Christmas, but not quite.

The air was cold – very, very cold. It was a raw, bitter, perishing cold which numbed fingers and toes, stung the skin on cheeks, and made it hurt to breathe. It was the sort of cold which made bones ache and lips turn blue.

On this sharp winter's night, the village of Brierley Bramble was quietly awaiting the arrival of dawn. By the frosted silver moonlight, the garden of 12 Oakfield Lane was a scene of fragile beauty. The frozen blades and stems of the garden had turned to delicate glass, ready to snap under the slightest weight.

In contrast, a warm glow came from the living-room window of number 12 itself. Inside, a family of four was enjoying an extremely early Christmas. Two young boys had woken their parents at 4am and were now playing with their brand-new gadgets, their eyes fixed upon their screens, their thumbs a blur of movement on the buttons. Their parents were the same, both transfixed by their even bigger, more expensive electronics.

Sadly, the festive joy was not shared by all at number 12, for back outside, down in one lonely corner of the long, frozen garden, sat a wooden hutch. It was the flimsy sort of hutch which pet shops often sold for guinea pigs. Inside was miserable. All the fresh hay had been eaten, whilst the few remaining strands were damp and flat. The food bowl was empty, save for a few husks of dried food, and the water bowl contained only stale, murky liquid.

In the damp, flat hay of the nesting box, three little guinea pigs huddled close to their mother for comfort and warmth. Poor Piggy Mama was doing her absolute best to keep her young ones warm, but her body shivered with the chill just as much as theirs. Her heart felt heavy as a stone as she held her young ones close. How she missed their father.

The eldest, Hazel, usually a bold character, bursting with plans and ideas, was now quietly pressed against Mama's side, subdued and lost in her own thoughts. Her brother, Alfie, was next. He had positioned himself so that their younger brother, Little Rufus, was tucked between him and Mama. Little Rufus snuggled down deep into the warmth of their fur.

The two young brothers were normally so mischievous, always up to silly boyish tricks, but there was no mischief in them today. Their small bellies ached with emptiness. They longed for some nice chunks of carrot, slices of apple or anything at all, just to stop the hunger pains. Their fun and fizz had disappeared as their energy slowly ebbed away.

It was not fair to blame the family at number 12. Admittedly, it was the boys' job to care for the guinea pigs, but Reggie had had football practice twice that week and detention for the rest of it, whilst Ronnie had a new video game which he was obsessed by, and he barely remembered to eat.

They may well have thought to clean out the guinea pigs at some point, and probably would have stuck a carrot or something in the cage if someone had just reminded them – but nobody did. Anyway, guinea pigs were pretty boring and didn't do anything entertaining at all. The boys had really wanted a dog.

As for their parents, they worked long hours and barely had time for their children, never mind some wretched rabbits or hamsters or whatever they were. They only bought the animals because all kids were supposed to have pets, weren't they? Didn't they teach them responsibility or something?

Everyone else's kids at Brierley Bramble Junior School seemed to have them, so the Brays just followed suit. They did not want a dog because that would have needed walking, and a cat might have scratched the furniture, so something to stick in a hutch in the garden seemed best.

The piggies had done everything they could think of to escape from their wooden prison. They had gnawed at the walls of the hutch, clawed at the door frame, and desperately tried to bite through the wire netting across it, but all their efforts had failed. Hazel had even hatched a daring plan to break out and escape, the next time one of the boys came along to open the hutch, but that had not happened for days. They were now getting weaker by the hour.

"If only Papa was here," whispered Alfie sadly.

Hazel heard him and swallowed hard. Piggy Papa had gone over the Rainbow Bridge just after Little Rufus was born, and the heartache was still raw.

Feeling the urge to be alone, Hazel left the other piggies, and crawled through to the front compartment of the hutch.

Despite the blast of icy air, she sat with her nose pressed against the cold wire netting of the door. She pressed as hard as she could, so it would hurt and stop her thinking about Piggy Papa. It did hurt, but it did not stop her painful thoughts.

She gazed up at the dark sky, softly lit by the Full Moon. The Moon gazed gently back at her. Hazel had always felt drawn to her luminous beauty, taking comfort from her nightly presence, even when a mere glimpse of her face was all the piggy could see. So often, Hazel had confided her hopes and dreams to the silver sphere, and felt she understood. The Moon and stars always stopped the darkness from filling her with fear.

But now, the darkness was closing in on the small guinea pig. She was weighed down by melancholy and full to the brim with despair. Was the inside of this drab wooden hutch all she would ever know? She knew nothing of the big wide world out there, a world she had always yearned to experience and explore. Now, it seemed as if she never would. Through hunger and cold, her life was about to end far sooner than it should. Hazel's eyes welled up, and the shapes in the frosty garden became a misty blur.

Yet... what was that?

Hazel blinked to clear her watery eyes and blinked again. A small silvery ball of light hovered in the garden, right before the hutch, just a short distance from Hazel's face. It was a soft, sparkling, gentle light, eerily exquisite in the darkness of the early morning. Hazel sat transfixed, unable to move. Whatever could it be? She should have been afraid yet was not. As she gazed at the silvery light, gentle waves of hope and warmth rippled slowly through her small body and melted her sadness at the edges. Thoughts of Piggy Papa filled her mind and made it seem like he was by her side.

Hazel wanted to hold it in her gaze forever, to reach out and touch it, but sadly, little by little, the bright orb of light faded until it disappeared from her sight. She blinked again, willing it to return, but it was gone. Had she imagined it? She wanted to call after

the orb and beg it to come back, but her voice failed her. She stared at the spot where it had been, her nose pressed once more against the icy wire, and shivered.

Meanwhile, hidden in the darkness of the garden, a pair of tiny yellow eyes blinked in the branches of a tree. Another pair of eyes appeared amongst the bushes, and that was joined by yet another. Further eyes appeared all around the garden. They waited and waited.

They were not the only ones keeping watch, for, next door to number 12, a pair of gentle blue eyes was also gazing from the window of number 14. A soft slightly wrinkled hand had pushed aside the curtain, and a kind face was peering out into the gloom.

Neither Ronnie, nor Reggie, nor their parents knew her name, even though they'd moved in over a year ago. She was just the strange old woman who lived in the cottage next door. They were particularly spooked by the way she wandered about her garden, calling for a cat that nobody had ever seen.

"I reckon she's a witch," Reggie declared.

"Or just nutty as a fruitcake!" scoffed Ronnie.

"Keep well away from her," their father had growled. "She's probably mentally unstable."

The boys had believed him. Any football sailing over the fence into their neighbour's garden was never retrieved. They avoided trick-or-treating at her cottage, and would have rather died than take any sponsored-walk forms round to *her* front door.

If they had ever bothered to ask, they would have found out her name was Betty Albright. She did not have a cat, but deliberately pretended she had, simply so they would think she was odd – it kept nuisances like Ronnie and Reggie away. For good measure, she kept a large old-fashioned broomstick outside her back door, just for effect.

Betty lived alone and was not celebrating Christmas this year. She'd had invitations from old friends in the village, like P.C. Frankie and his wife, but she had politely declined each one, preferring to spend Christmas Day with the memories of her late husband, Harry, in the comfort of her own home.

Besides, she had sprained her ankle on the icy pavement, and had been hobbling around painfully for the past few days, so it was all too much effort to do anything festive, especially now Harry was gone. Her only comfort was his old walking stick, which was helping her get about as best she could.

Despite it being the early hours of the morning, Betty was up and awake, as usual. She had been preparing a turmeric poultice for her swollen ankle, and was now glancing out of her kitchen window, to see what sort of weather the day might bring. She liked to keep a watchful eye on the birds, foxes, and other wildlife, which frequented her garden.

Somehow, Betty had an odd feeling that something was not quite right. As she peered into the garden, something strange caught her eye. Taking her walking stick in one hand, before slipping on her big baggy cardigan, Betty unlocked her back door and looked out for a better view. She rubbed her eyes and looked again. No, she was not mistaken; she definitely saw a strange silvery ball of light hovering in the air before her. Was it a trick? Was it something to do with those boys next door?

For some reason, she didn't feel afraid as she slowly hobbled forward in her slippers. She hardly noticed the sharp chill in the air, as the orb of light seemed to give off a sensation of warmth and happiness. It made her think of green fields, of sunshine and of Harry.

Betty gazed at the light and found herself following it down the garden. Through the darkness she went, her furry slippers crunching on the frosty grass as she limped along. Next thing she knew, she was standing at her neighbour's fence.

Hidden from view, behind a large bush, some of the wooden panels had weakened and loosened, leaving a space just big enough to slip through. After hesitating slightly, Betty followed the orb as it led her through the gap and into the garden of number 12.

With her focus on the light, and nothing else, she did not see the many, many pairs of eyes which were watching from the bushes and the trees around her.

She looked around the unfamiliar garden, lit by the moon. A strange sense of purpose seemed to possess her. She felt as though she had a job to do, without knowing quite what –

until that is, her gaze fell upon the lonely wooden hutch. Some instinct made her take a closer look.

She shuffled forward and caught sight of something small and furry pressed against the wire netting at the front. Betty bent down to investigate further, and a pair of desperate eyes met hers. A wave of anger swept over her as she saw the sparse hay and empty food bowl, behind the small frame of Hazel, the guinea pig.

As quickly as her painful ankle would allow, Betty reached around the hutch and fumbled for the catch. It was stiff with the frost and hard to budge, but, after a bash with her walking stick, Betty defeated the metal hook and knocked open the hutch door. Hazel's small furry face stared out, startled.

Not for long. As soon as Hazel looked up into the kind blue eyes of Betty, she knew instinctively there was no danger. This was their chance. Their prison had finally been broken open. Coming to her senses, she called to the others, "Mama! Alfie! Rufus! We're free!"

All Betty heard was the excited *wheeking* noise that guinea pigs make, and did not know what to think, until four overjoyed animals leapt out of the hutch and onto the frozen grass by her feet. She laughed and clapped her hands to see the four furry little bodies tumbling over each other in excitement.

But – all excitement stopped in a heartbeat.

Some distance away, at the top of the garden, the back

door of number 12 had been flung open wide. A deep booming voice bellowed out, "Hey! Who's there?"

Betty froze.

She tried to stammer out an explanation, but her throat had tightened in panic, leaving her unable to speak. Two big windows had now been thrown open too, and more angry faces had appeared.

Mr Bray, Ronnie and Reggie's father, began to stride down the garden, like an angry steam engine.

In desperation, Betty turned to search for the light which had led her there and saw, for the first time, the many, many pairs of eyes blinking in the darkness around her. Had she been able to gasp, she would have done so, but now, as if things could not get any worse, the eyes seemed to be moving, and moving closer. They seemed to be moving directly towards *her*.

They were *indeed* moving towards her, and, picking up speed, extremely fast.

Betty breathed in hard. There was no time to escape.

Now, out of the gloom, came a sudden scurrying of many, many paws and tiny feet, and a flapping of many, many wings.

There was screeching and howling, hissing and growling, as a mass of furry bodies and feathery wings rushed towards her. She instinctively covered her face and awaited the attack. At her feet, the four small guinea pigs were paralysed with fear.

However, the army of fur and feathers kept advancing, sweeping straight past Betty and the piggies, straight up the frozen garden, straight up towards the house, straight past Mr Bray, and straight through the open doors and windows of number 12.

Mr Bray shrieked and fled back into the house. High-pitched screams of horror rang out into the cold early morning air. The Brays, inside, did not know what had hit them. Within seconds, there were owls and pigeons circling around their living room ceiling; foxes romping over their chairs and settees; weasels and stoats scrambling up their curtains; badgers dashing around their kitchen floor, and squirrels scampering over their shiny work surfaces. It was pure pandemonium.

Betty stared at number 12 with her mouth open wide, in sheer disbelief. What on earth...?

Her attention, however, was drawn back by the reappearance of the silvery orb, close by her cheek. This time it had company; four more lights, of different colours and hue, were gently twinkling around her, as if to calm and reassure. Like the silvery orb, they were small, round and beautiful, floating in the murky air. Their intense beauty dissolved Betty's fear in an instant, leaving her full of calm wonder.

At her feet, the piggies felt exactly the same. Like most small animals, when faced with extreme danger, they had frozen like mini statues, but now, as they watched the pretty lights, their tiny heartbeats stopped thumping just quite so hard, and they found themselves able to breathe once more.

Somehow, despite the chaos, Betty understood that this was her one chance to save the guinea pigs, without having to face the family at number 12. Ignoring the screeching and screaming still coming from the house, she scooped up Little Rufus, and popped him into one of her cardigan pockets. She did the same to Alfie. Hazel and Piggy Mama were placed inside her cardigan and cradled against her shoulder. Despite the pain from her ankle, she was desperate to get the guinea pigs to safety, so she limped back to the gap in the fence as quickly as she could.

Back across her own frozen lawn she limped, over her house step, and finally back into the safety of her kitchen, where Betty slammed the door shut and locked it. She stole a nervous glance out of the window. The orbs could still be seen hovering over the garden of number 12, as animals of every shape and size scrambled out of the house and disappeared back into the night.

"Well I never!" she exclaimed to the little piggies as she gently set each one of them down upon the floor. "Well I never did, I'm sure!"

It took a few minutes for Betty to process what had just happened out there in the back garden. When she finally got her thoughts in order, she looked down at the four little furry faces looking expectantly back, "Now, whatever am I going to do with you?"

She thought back fondly to the two guinea pigs she'd had as a young girl, then sprang into action as quickly as she could. The first thing they needed was food and warmth, so a soft clean towel in a large strong cardboard box became a makeshift home. Betty placed it on the floor of the warm kitchen, in front of the open wood fire with its soothing flames. The piggies waited patiently, as each in turn was gently cupped in Betty's warm hands and placed inside the box. An early breakfast was soon provided and the famished piggies feasted hungrily on delicious celery leaves and wedges of carrot, washed down with the most wonderful fresh cool water.

As they tucked in, Betty gently inspected them for injuries. Finding Little Rufus had a cut foot, she bathed it with warm salt water and sprinkled on a little powdered yarrow to help it heal.

The four little piggies ate and ate until they could manage no more, before settling down comfortably in their warm cardboard box, hardly able to believe what had just happened to them that Christmas morning. They might have wondered why Betty appeared as she did, and why all those pretty lights had twinkled around them in the semi-darkness, but they did not have the energy. With their bellies full and the wonderful warmth of the kitchen surrounding them, their heavy eyes soon shut.

Betty smiled as she tickled each piggy around the ear, and smoothed their fur with her soft hand, before settling down with a much-needed cup of tea. Had she, ordinary Betty Albright, really just followed a mysterious silver light into next door's garden, and stolen her neighbours' guinea pigs? She chuckled to herself in disbelief. Looking up at her husband's picture on the wall, she wondered how many laws she had just broken and what Harry would have said.

Drifting off to sleep, Hazel snuggled up next to Alfie, Little Rufus and Mama, feeling the same disbelief. What was that strange ball of light? She longed to gaze upon its beauty once more and feel its warmth. She was so sure it had just saved their lives. How she wished... but her tired eyes were soon closing. Then she dreamed the sweetest dreams of silver lights and Piggy Papa.

Little did she know, life still had much, much more in store for one small guinea pig.

Chapter 2
Mr Bray

THE family at number 12 sat in a stupor, each member staring straight ahead, too dazed to speak. A single small white feather floated gently down from the ceiling and landed silently in the hair of Mrs Bray. Not that she noticed, nor did it matter, for she and the rest of her family had the same wild windswept look, with remnants of feather and fur clinging to their faces and clothes.

Mr Bray sat twitching, the few sensible thoughts he was capable of thinking, having deserted him. His wife and sons sat without even blinking.

A scene of chaos surrounded them; cushions had burst, chairs had been upended, vases lay broken, pictures dangled from walls, and lampshades hung at strange angles.

Somewhere in the room, an electronic device was pinging, but no one seemed to notice.

Eventually, Mrs Bray got to her feet. In a trance-like state, she wandered into the kitchen. She returned, moments later, with a roll of black bin bags. She absent-mindedly tore one off, without emotion, and began filling it with debris from around the room, too shocked to allow herself to actually contemplate what had just happened.

Her movements seemed to bring the others in the room back to their senses. Reggie began to giggle in a slightly hysterical way, his body convulsing with each breath.

Ronnie looked around in disbelief. Struggling to speak, he asked, "W-what just happened...?" He looked to his father for an answer.

Mr Bray gawped back at him like a goldfish, doing his best to look like he had the faintest clue. His eyes searched around the room for answers, his brain trying hard to interpret the scene of devastation around him. In time, he stood up and did what he always did best – got angry.

He needed someone to blame, someone to shout at. He drew in an enormous breath and whipped out his phone. Ferociously, he jabbed at the handset with an angry finger. He did not need to look up the number of the local police station, as he was very well used to ringing it.

As he blurted out an account of events at his home, into the ear of whichever unfortunate desk sergeant was on duty this time, he felt yet more anger. *Yes*, he informed them, it *was* 'their old friend, Mr Bray', and yes, he was *fully* aware it was Christmas Day, and indeed, wild animals really *had* invaded his home.

He did not bother to carry on. He got the distinct impression that others in the police station had been invited to listen in on the call, and he was more than convinced that he could hear something resembling sniggering.

Meanwhile, back at number 14, Hazel opened her eyes and took a deep blissful breath. The soft warm towel beneath her cheek reassured her that she was no longer in the cold wooden hutch with the damp flat hay. Alfie and Little Rufus were close by her feet, while Mama was only breathing distance away.

How long had she been asleep? Grey feeble daylight could be seen through the kitchen window as she stretched and yawned, accidentally jolting Alfie awake with her foot. He would have complained, but he was so comfortable and content that he merely turned over and snoozed a little more.

Betty was dozing in the chair close by. Hazel could just see her over the rim of the cardboard box, and let out a small friendly *wheek* as if to say hello.

Betty's eyes opened immediately. Seeing Hazel's tiny pink nose by the edge of the box, she smiled. "Why, hello, my dear," she said cheerfully. "Have you had a good sleep?"

At the sound of her gentle voice, Mama, Alfie and Little Rufus woke too, stretching and yawning comfortably on the soft towel.

Betty shuffled over to the box and gave each piggy a little

tickle around the ear, plus a quick rub under the chin. She thought to herself what handsome creatures they were.

Hazel had attractive white patches on lively red-brown fur. Alfie was the same brown, but the white on him was limited to a crest of fur which stood on end between his ears and matched the pale rims he had around his eyes. Mama was a darker, rich brown colour, broken up by small flecks of a different shade, which also coloured the fur on her underside. Little Rufus was pure white, apart from a patch of red-brown over one eye.

Betty thought back to Sally and Titch, the guinea pigs she'd had as a child, and remembered how much they loved to be given the freedom of a big space, to stretch their legs and poke about. One by one, she lifted the piggies out of the box and placed them down upon the carpet. First Hazel, then Alfie, then Piggy Mama, and finally, Little Rufus.

At first, the piggies were a little anxious and too afraid to move. They were so used to being cooped up in the hutch that this new experience was too strange. What was happening?

Betty looked at them huddled up together, right next to the box, and smiled sympathetically at their reluctance to move. She crossed over to her windowsill, where fresh parsley grew in a pot, and picked out a few stalks. She tore them up into small pieces, and then scattered them over different parts of the floor, laying a trail leading right up to the piggies.

Hazel understood immediately. She leapt forward to the first piece of parsley and gobbled it up, "Come on!" she wheeked to the others, before trotting off to explore and stretch her legs.

Alfie and Little Rufus were never slow when anything to eat was on offer, so they soon scampered after their sister, sniffing out the bits of green herb and feasting on each delicious morsel they could find. Piggy Mama finally joined in too.

With each step, the piggies' confidence increased. They loved this sensation of freedom; it felt so good to use their legs properly and move more than just the width of the dreaded hutch. In time, they began to pick up speed and genuinely enjoy themselves, scuttling around the legs of the table and chairs, exploring every nook and cranny of the kitchen.

Betty watched their tiny feet disappearing in and out of the furniture and chuckled. They reminded her of little hippos with their round back ends. She loved to watch their ears fluttering at the edges, like soft little cornflakes, as they scurried about the kitchen floor.

Once all the parsley was gone, and the piggies had run out of energy, Betty retrieved each one and placed them back in their box.

Inside the Brays' house, some semblance of normality had been restored. The cracked, broken or burst items had been removed and everything else put back where it belonged. Mrs Bray had somehow still cooked a Christmas meal (of sorts) amidst the mayhem, and the family had finally sat down to eat. They were now slumped in front of the television screen, too tired to know what they were watching.

Mr Bray eventually found the energy to go out into the garden, and look for clues which might possibly explain the strange events, which had taken place in the early hours of the morning. He was still smarting from the unsympathetic response of the local police, and had decided to carry out his own investigation.

It was only as he prowled around the end of the garden, that Mr Bray happened to discover the disappearance of the family's guinea pigs. When this outrage was finally noticed, and reported to those inside, the Brays had to think hard. When did this terrible thing happen? When had they last seen them? Whose turn had it been to throw some food into the hutch? No one could remember.

They assured themselves it was not their fault. After all, they'd had to deal with a brutal wild animal attack that morning. Who could think straight when traumatised?

Anyway, it didn't matter *when* it had happened. The point was that something of theirs had clearly been stolen.

Eric Bray was a big, angry man, used to getting his own way. The world was always against him and he was always ready to yell aggressively at it until it caved in, which it frequently did, just to get some peace and quiet and be rid of him.

Now he had yet another injustice to deal with. He had never actually liked the things that lived in the hutch. In fact, he could not actually remember what they looked like, but the point was they *belonged* to him and his family. The things were *their* possessions, and somebody else was possessing them.

He and the boys walked around the empty hutch, inspecting the bent catch at the side. Their gaze then fell upon something lying in the long grass behind it. Something which did not belong there. Mr Bray seized the offending item and brandished it in the air before the faces of Ronnie and Reggie.

"A walking stick!" exclaimed Ronnie as he saw it. "Has someone *old* been in our garden?"

"Who do we know that's *old?*" asked Reggie.

The exact same thought dawned on each boy at the exact same time. The brothers stared at each other, wide-eyed in horror.

"Do you think it's that old witch's, from next door?" Reggie gasped.

"Are you sure it's not a broom stick?" Ronnie spluttered.

Mr Bray drew in an angry breath. He wanted to storm right round to that woman's front door and batter on it till she answered, but he was actually rather afraid of her. She was plainly mad, possibly even a witch, and he was not keen on going near some dangerous old woman, especially now the daylight was fading fast, and it was becoming dark once more.

This was a dilemma. Much as he did not want to go next door, he could not lose face in front of his children. He puffed up his chest, breathed in hard, and slowly walked up the garden. "I'll deal with this, boys," he announced quietly between gritted teeth.

"Yeah, Dad!" chorused Ronnie and Reggie, loving the aggressive look on his face. Little did they realise it was merely nerves keeping his jaws firmly clamped shut.

To play for time (and gather his courage) Mr Bray went inside to wrap a large protective red scarf around his neck. Aware his sons were watching him intently, he paused to scrape away an imaginary lump of dirt from his coat sleeve. This seemed to take rather a long time. He did, however, finally turn the handle of the door and step out into the street.

All too soon for his liking, he found himself standing on Betty's doorstep, his hand poised, ready to knock. He was only hesitating, he told himself, because he needed to think of what to say. As always, he decided aggression was the best policy, so he pounded on the door with the edge of his fist in an intimidating manner.

Inside number 14, the piggies each jumped in fright at the harsh sound booming through the house. Betty sat up, startled at the noise. She knew all too well who that might be. Still, better get it over with. She got to her feet, wincing slightly at the pain in her ankle, and limped out, into the hallway, ready to face the music.

Betty did not like conflict, but she knew that the best way to deal with bullies was to confront them head on. So, she took a deep breath, and pulled open the door to see Mr Bray standing there, with a face as red as the scarf wound around his neck.

"Yes?" she asked politely. Betty could not help noticing him flinch slightly as she spoke. Indeed, he hesitated just that second too long before blurting out, "What have you done with our hamsters!"

"Hamsters?" she asked in genuine surprise. "What hamsters?"

"The ones from the hutch in our garden!"

Betty immediately sensed she had the upper hand in this conversation, and gained a little confidence. "No one keeps hamsters outside in a hutch," she replied calmly.

"I *meant* rabbits," fumed Mr Bray, as he winced at his mistake.

"Dad!" called Reggie, who was listening from the safety of his bedroom window, next door. "They're guinea pigs!"

Mr Bray stared at Betty in frustration and simply uttered, "I meant *guinea pigs*," through his tight lips.

Betty was beginning to feel genuine anger with this buffoon of a man. He clearly cared little for the poor animals. She spoke slowly, frequently swallowing hard to contain the rage slowly building inside her.

"Guinea pigs, you say. You had guinea pigs...out in a hutch in your garden... in this weather?" she asked. "The temperature, at the moment, is near freezing... It has been for days... yet... you are telling me that you left some poor little creatures out there to suffer?"

Mr Bray was lost for words. He was supposed to be accusing *her* of a crime, but now it seemed she was accusing *him* of one instead. He did not know how to handle this new situation. The best he could manage was a huffy, "What have you done with them?"

Ignoring this, Betty carried on, sharply, "Small animals *must* be taken inside during the winter! Didn't you know that?"

"No!" shot back Mr Bray, his mind unable to come up with anything better.

"Did you even bother to read up on guinea pigs before you bought them?" snapped Betty.

"Do what?" spluttered Mr Bray. This conversation was becoming bizarre.

"Didn't you think to go to the library and get a book out on keeping guinea pigs?!"

The words 'book' and 'library' stunned Mr Bray into silence. Whatever was the crazy old bat talking about? Why would he *ever* go near either of those two things?

Unsure of how to respond at this point, he resorted to his other favourite tactic of abuse. "You silly old... old... *witch!*"

Betty now realised just why he was so hesitant. Ha, ha, the trick, with the imaginary black cat and broomstick, had worked. No problem, she could use this childish insult to her advantage. She brought her eyebrows down low over her eyes and began to hum.

As she did so, the silvery orb, from the early hours of that morning, suddenly reappeared, behind her. It hovered just over Betty's shoulder and sparkled gently. She did not see it, but Mr Bray certainly did, and nearly choked on his own tongue.

He stared in amazement as four small multi-coloured lights began floating around the crown of Betty's head, like a halo.

By now, Betty had lost all fear of her bullish next-door

neighbour. She had seen through his bluster, and decided to have a little enjoyment at his expense.

Just behind the door, was her feather duster. Keeping her eyes firmly on Mr Bray, she reached out her hand, and plucked out a bright yellow feather from it. Continuing to hum, she held the yellow plume between her forefinger and thumb, and pointed it towards him. As she did so, she chanted over his head, with an intense look upon her face,

"By the power of Hecate, I call upon thee..."

Mr Bray went deathly white. The old hag was casting a spell! She really was a witch!

"... I call upon thee... oh, woodland creatures... to come to me this twilight hour..." Betty continued, in a slow, hypnotic tone.

Woodland creatures? Mr Bray almost screamed. It had been her all along! *She* had made all those wild beasts invade his house that morning!

He jumped backwards in a complete panic, lost his balance and ended up as a heap on the ground. Immediately, he scrambled to his feet, clambered straight over the low dividing wall between the houses, stumbled up the steps to his own front door, clawed it open, and fell through to safety.

With violently shaking hands, he snatched the phone from his pocket, stabbed at the handset, and screamed a garbled jumble of words into the device,

"Mr Bray again... Oakfield Lane... Another attack... old woman... weird lights... evil spirits... yellow feathers..."

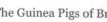

The same desk sergeant as before raised his eyes to the heavens and silently gestured to his colleagues nearby to listen in on the call.

This time, Mr Bray was absolutely sure, he heard not just sniggering, but absolute hysterics.

Chapter 3
A Difficult Decision

INSIDE Betty's kitchen, the piggies had nervously huddled together in their box, as the all-too-familiar voice of Mr Bray had come booming down the hallway, from outside.

They felt deep fear. Was he coming in to get them? Were they going back to the cold damp hutch? Their hearts lurched as the door to the kitchen burst open. They shut their eyes and buried their heads in each other's fur, but to their huge relief, it was Betty who came through. She immediately sat down in her chair, covered her face with her hands, and laughed, and laughed.

The laughter was slightly hysterical. It was a mixture of immense relief at the end of her confrontation with Mr Bray and pure amusement at the stupidity of the man. She laughed till the tears streamed down her face. Betty took her hands away and looked up at the picture of her husband on the wall. "Well, I never, Harry! I reckon you'd have been proud of me there!"

As her laughter subsided, she noticed the four small anxious faces looking up at her from their cardboard home. Betty knelt down, as best she could. "Don't worry, my dears," she said softly, as she tickled their ears, "I don't think we'll be hearing from him again in a hurry."

And so, the rest of the festive season passed peacefully. The piggies grew happier each day, feeling warm, safe and secure. They now trusted Betty completely and would often 'talk' to her, wheeking loudly for their breakfast each morning.

Little Rufus, especially, would be the loudest, wheeking as if he'd not eaten for a week. He had not forgotten his ordeal at number 12, and was frequently worried that he would be left to starve again.

When it was time for their run, Betty would plant small chunks of carrot, thin slivers of apple, plus the occasional strand of sweet-tasting parsley around the floor, tucked away here and there to create a mini treasure hunt.

Hazel would always be straight out of the box to stretch her legs and just enjoy the freedom, whilst Alfie and Little Rufus would run around, competing with each other to find the hidden treats first. Alfie was frequently the quickest, much to his younger brother's annoyance. All too often, it would finish

with the brothers squabbling
and bickering, with their
teeth chattering together, as
annoyed piggies do, until
Piggy Mama scolded them
and put a stop to it.

Each time, Betty would sit
back with a cup of tea, watching their
antics with a big beam on her face. She
loved to see Piggy Mama taking her
time, nibbling on the odd chunk of
carrot, but mostly keeping a close eye on
her children.

She loved too, the sight of Alfie and Little Rufus racing
around, chattering and wheeking at each other. But, most of
all, she loved to watch Hazel, with her constant curiosity and
urge to explore. The little piggy did occasionally pause to eat,
when she found a tasty chunk of something, but it was never
her main purpose. She was much more interested in
investigating every inch of the kitchen, sniffing out new
smells and discovering new places.

Betty could sense that there was something rather special
about this little guinea pig. As the days passed, a deep bond
was slowly forming between the two of them.

Betty was not a great sleeper, not since she'd lost Harry.
She would often stay awake well into the late evening, sitting
in her rocking chair, in her cosy kitchen, with the wood fire

burning. The flames would flicker and dance in the dim light, providing calming warmth. At such times, Betty would often notice Hazel sitting awake too, whilst the other three piggies slept soundly.

Betty would gently lift the little piggy out, and sit her on her lap. The two then enjoyed each other's company, both thinking their own thoughts. Frequently, as if in harmony with each other, those thoughts would linger on that mysterious silver orb they'd both seen in the early hours of Christmas morning. Both had felt deeply affected by it, and both had longed to see it once more.

One evening, Betty and Hazel sat in the rocking chair, gazing into the fire. Betty was deep in thought. She had truly grown to love the family of guinea pigs, enjoying their companionship more and more each day. She loved their impatient cheeky wheeking for food, and even enjoyed the five-minute chase it took to get Alfie and Little Rufus back into their box, when exercise time was over – exhausting though it was. The four small creatures delighted her heart more than she could put into words.

However, a thought was nagging away at her. Much as she loved them, they could not stay with her forever. Guinea pigs needed fresh air and green grass. They needed the chance to run around a nice sunny garden. That could never happen with the Brays next door, and she could never be sure they wouldn't try to take them back.

It broke her heart to admit it, but she needed to find them

a new home – a home which suited them and gave them all they needed. Once the New Year was over, Betty would start her search. There was no rush she told herself.

For now, she had to make sure the guinea pigs were as well looked after as possible. It was time to get some proper provisions in for them. They couldn't live off fruit and vegetables alone; they needed nice fresh hay and proper dried food. Her ankle was on the mend, so a shopping trip into the village was not out of the question, but she still needed the support of her walking stick to feel totally confident in venturing out.

There was just one problem – her walking stick was still next door.

After finding it in his garden, Mr Bray had tried to snap it, but wasn't strong enough. He had considered sawing it in half, but that would have required some effort, plus he didn't have any tools, so he'd just taken his temper out on it by whacking it about and kicking it. He'd managed to dent it and bend it a bit, and generally mess it up, which pleased him. He was then going to throw it over the mad woman's fence but, like a true coward, he was scared that she'd see his spiteful actions as a reason to put another curse on him. Instead, he stuck it in the bin, at the front of his garden, to be taken away with the rubbish.

From her window, Betty had spotted Harry's faithful old stick poking out from under the bin lid. As there were no rubbish collections due for a while, she waited patiently for a time when her neighbours would not be at home. The time finally came when Betty heard their voices emerging from their front door – the Brays never did anything quietly. She watched from behind her front curtains as the family piled into their car and zoomed off down the street, with Mr Bray driving, as always, like he owned the road.

Betty seized her opportunity and popped out of her door, as quickly as her ankle would allow, before limping round to her neighbours' front garden. Without delay, she lifted the bin lid and retrieved the precious walking stick. Knowing Mr Bray as she did, she was not surprised to find it damaged. She sighed deeply, feeling just a little tearful at the way her dear husband's stick had suffered at his hands. That is, until an idea crossed her mind. It was time to have a little more fun at Mr Bray's expense.

She hobbled back into her cottage, and brought back a few more yellow feathers, plucked from her duster – like the one she'd held up to Mr Bray during their altercation on her doorstep, on Christmas Day. Smiling at the memory of his terrified expression, Betty placed the feathers carefully onto the lid of his bin, and weighed them down with a stone, making sure they could easily be seen.

Later that day, when the Bray family returned home, Betty could not resist peeking out again, from behind her front curtains. As they clambered out of the car, Ronnie and Reggie were squabbling as usual, Mr Bray was shouting at them as usual, and as usual, his wife was texting on her phone. All normal activity was suspended however, as their eyes simultaneously fell upon the yellow feathers, placed so carefully upon the bin. Silence reigned for a few glorious seconds as each Bray blinked and stared at them.

"More witchcraft!" shrieked Mr Bray.

Chaos then descended as each family member screamed and fell over each other to be the first one up their front door step, and into their home.

Later that evening, as Betty and Hazel sat once more by the fire, Betty could not help chuckling to herself at the memory of it all. As the flames grew smaller with the passing of time, she drifted off into a deep sleep, with a smile still playing upon her lips.

Whilst Betty and Hazel slumbered peacefully, little did they know that the mysterious silver orb was still watching over them. It hovered gently around their heads, and twinkled gently in the stillness of the night.

Chapter 4
Billy Greenwood

As the new calendar year finally got under way, life returned to normal in Brierley Bramble. The Christmas decorations had been taken down, and fairy lights no longer cheered the various cottage windows. Bleary-eyed villagers returned to early morning starts, the shops opened their doors for business once more, and reluctant children returned to school.

Fortunately for all, the sun had decided to emerge from behind the clouds that morning, to create a bright crisp winter's day.

Betty was up early, as always. Cheered by the weather, she intended to take her first trip out since Christmas.

After providing breakfast for the hungry piggies, she set off to the village, pulling her trolley bag on wheels behind her. She walked slowly to allow for her slightly delicate ankle, supported by her rather battered walking stick.

Down the road Betty strolled, breathing in the sunshine, and feeling glad to be alive as she passed the open fields. The sunny day had lifted the winter gloom from all around her.

Eventually, she entered the centre of the village, where she passed along the row of multi-coloured shops: from the baker's, the post office and the greengrocer's, to the newsagent's, the cobbler's and the florist's. From each doorway or window, a friendly face smiled and waved hello. Betty waved happily back, recognising every face.

Finally, she stopped at the hardware store owned by Ernie Bostock. A gentle shop bell tinkled as she opened the door and stepped inside. The interior was an Aladdin's cave of domestic items. Ernie sold all sorts: from screwdrivers, fuse wire, hot water bottles and air fresheners, to brooms, washing lines, garden plants and pet supplies. There were items on shelves as high as the eye could see, items hanging from the walls and the ceiling, and items stacked up on the counter. Indeed, every inch of the shop was taken up with items for sale, yet Ernie knew exactly where everything was, and could locate anything required in seconds.

"Good morning, Betty!" he beamed. "A Happy New Year to you."

"And to you, Ernie," smiled Betty. "I need your very best dry guinea pig food please."

Meanwhile, in another part of Brierley Bramble, a young boy named Billy Greenwood was sitting in class, lost in his own thoughts. The Christmas holidays now seemed an age away. He had given up listening to the teacher some time ago, as he simply did not care about spotting the clauses in a sentence. He cared even less about the nouns and the adjectives, the verbs and the adverbials.

On a beautiful sunny day like today, he did not want to be cooped up in this classroom, on a hard-plastic chair, behind a hard-plastic desk. He wanted to be outside in the fresh clean air. He wanted to be running through meadows and climbing trees. He wanted to be digging holes and looking for worms, or lifting up stones and counting woodlice. He wanted to be in the woods, searching for squirrel dreys, or laying low to watch for badgers and foxes.

Billy was a highly intelligent boy, but he disliked school. He had an expert knowledge of animals, and could tell a person anything they ever wanted to know about the life cycle of a wasp, the hibernation habits of a dormouse or the preferred diet of a great crested newt. He knew everything there was to know about house spiders and why it was so wrong to kill them.

He could draw pencil sketches of woodland creatures in breath-taking detail, and recite endless poems about wolves, lone dogs and adventurous cats, but these skills seemed to be of no use at all in the modern education system.

Billy was required to sit still and listen. Each day, he was required to sit still in assembly, to sit still for the literacy hour and to sit still for numeracy. He had to pass tests and meet his personal targets. The tests were absolutely *essential* to his future, his young, fresh-faced teacher stated. Could he really face the shame of low data scores?

No, she told him, sharply, he could *not* bring in insects or tell the rest of the class about the beauty of earthworms. Yes, she *was* sure that pipistrelle bats were incredibly interesting creatures, but they would *not* help him with his schoolwork. He really *had* to focus more on the text in front of him, and answer the questions set.

By break time, Billy had had enough. Whilst the other children kicked around a football or played hopscotch, he dodged the teacher on duty and made his way to the back of the school building. There he found the tall beech tree, with a branch that hung low over the side of the perimeter fence. Billy had his escape route down to a fine art. Using his finely-honed climbing skills, he was soon up the tree, over the fence and off to freedom.

From her office window, Mrs Kinder, the school headteacher, watched him go with a resigned sigh. As she lifted the phone to ring his father, yet again, she glanced at her computer screen with its ghastly spread sheet of numbers. Just two terms away from retirement and counting off the days, she understood only too well his urge to be free. For two pins, she'd kick off her shoes and disappear over the fence herself.

Back in the local hardware store, Betty had finished chatting with Ernie, and was stepping out of the doorway, with her shopping trolley full of hay and dried food.

As she walked along, walking stick in hand, she thought about the four guinea pigs waiting for her at home, and imagined how happy they'd be to taste fresh sweet meadow hay.

The thought of this, along with the bright sunny day, made her feel so chirpy, yet the thorny problem of finding the small animals a new home was always at the back of her mind, niggling away. She thought about it all the way back through the village, and all the way along the road which led to home.

As she passed by the fields, Betty noticed a small figure hunched up at the roadside. It was clearly a child, and as she got closer, Betty recognised the tousled brown hair of

Billy Greenwood, who seemed to be cradling something in his arms.

Billy always made her smile. He was one of those children who somehow looked dishevelled and untidy, no matter how well they were dressed by their parents. Billy's hair always stood on end at the crown, refusing to settle down and look respectable. His trousers were usually crumpled, and his shirt collar was regularly askew, whilst his jumper generally looked like he'd crawled under a hedge whilst wearing it — which he frequently had.

All the villagers had a soft spot for him, especially as he'd lost his mother, Isabella, a couple of years before. She'd been a Scots girl, from Perth, who had met and married his father, John, after a holiday romance had turned to deep heartfelt love. All who knew her were devastated by her loss. Billy and his teenage sister, Molly, were now being brought up, single-handedly, by their dad.

As she neared the figure, Betty called out to him, "Hello, Billy! Not in school again? What have you got there?"

Billy raised his head and looked forlornly up at her, "It's a young magpie, Betty. I found him under the hedge. He's hurt his wing and can't fly"

"Oh dear," replied Betty in a low voice. "Can I see?"

Billy got carefully to his feet and turned so Betty could view the bird nestled against his chest. It had indeed got a wing which didn't quite hang as it should.

"Don't you worry," Betty told him in a reassuring voice,

"your dad will sort that little fellow out, just like he always does."

The magpie merely blinked and settled back, seemingly unafraid as Billy gently stroked his finger along its head and neck.

Betty knew that his dad, John Greenwood, would work his usual magic with the latest injured animal brought home by Billy. He was the local master carpenter, a gifted wood craftsman (from generations of the same) who always had a smile on his face and a kind word for everyone.

She'd been so sad for him when he had lost his wife. He'd always been considered quite a catch by the local village girls, with his shiny chestnut hair and velvety brown eyes. Many had thought he'd look to replace the first Mrs Greenwood at some point, but there was little sign of that. He was too firmly focused on his children and his work.

Betty glanced up to see the very man himself, now pulling up at the roadside, in his truck. "Hello, Betty," he said, rolling down the window. "I see a certain boy is out of school — again."

Betty grinned as she watched him raise his eyebrows quizzically at his son, as if to ask what the problem was this time.

Billy looked up at his father and indicated the bird in his arms. "He's hurt, Dad."

Mr Greenwood knew full well why his son usually broke out of school, so didn't bother pressing him to explain any further. Instead, he climbed out of his vehicle to have a look at the latest animal patient.

"We'll soon fix him," he reassured Billy. "Let's get him in a box and make him comfortable."

Opening up the back of his truck, he produced a suitable box, with some soft material in the bottom. He was always well equipped to deal with whatever Billy found next. He cupped his strong hands around the magpie and placed it tenderly into the container, before carefully setting it down in the back of the truck.

"Right, now we'd best get you back to school."

Billy's face fell.

"Don't worry," said his dad, "I've spoken to Mrs Kinder. It's art and P.E. this afternoon – you like those. Now hop in."

As his son clambered into the truck, Mr Greenwood turned his attention to Betty, "Can we give you a lift home, Betty?"

"No, don't trouble yourself, John, I'll be there soon enough," she smiled, resting on her walking stick.

Mr Greenwood's eye fell upon the battered stick. His face grew concerned. "Well, that's seen better days! Whatever's happened there?"

"Oh, it's a long story," laughed Betty. "It does me well enough."

"Nonsense, Betty," he insisted, "let's take a closer look."

Mr Greenwood took the wooden walking stick and inspected it from all angles. "I think your stick needs just as much attention as the poor bird," he finally pronounced. "Let's get you into the truck too, Betty. I'll take this into my workshop and see what I can do."

As she went to protest, he raised his palm, "No buts, Betty, come along."

Within minutes, Betty's shopping was loaded into the back of the truck, and Billy had budged up on the wide front seat to make room for her.

After dropping Billy off at the school gates (to be safely escorted back in by Mrs Kinder) Betty and John were soon trundling along the road, heading for the Greenwood house on the edge of the village.

The Greenwood's home was an old Georgian farmhouse, surrounded by meadows. It was known as 'Bowood' and generations of Greenwoods had lived there for longer than anyone could remember. The house was situated on the very edge of Brierley Bramble, and was accessed from the road by a long dirt track.

After John Greenwood's truck had made its way along this very track, Betty was helped down from the vehicle, and escorted through the house, into the roomy kitchen. Minutes later, she was seated on a comfy chair, sipping from a nice hot mug of tea.

Despite the sunshine, it was still a cold day, so she was glad to be near the old Aga stove, which gave off such a strong steady heat. Mr Greenwood then disappeared into his workshop in the garden, taking both the magpie and Betty's stick, leaving her to admire the view from the large kitchen window.

As Betty sipped her tea, a fluffy little dog came padding in to sit by her feet. It held its head up proudly by Betty's knee, clearly expecting to be stroked. Betty looked down at the furry head, "Hello, Madam Pom," she said fondly. She often met the dignified little Pomeranian being walked by Billy or John, and always stopped to tickle her around the fox-like ears.

Whilst she fondled the soft head, a thought was slowly growing in Betty's mind. A tiny seed of an idea had planted itself earlier, as she'd watched Billy nursing the injured magpie in his arms. Now it had firmly taken root. This home was owned by a kind animal-loving family, who she knew well, with plenty of space and a very pleasant safe back garden.

After some time, there had been no sign of John Greenwood, so Betty steadied herself on her weak ankle, and walked slowly over to the door leading out into the back. Accompanied by the small Pomeranian, she lifted the latch, stepped out and looked around.

It had been a while since she'd visited Bowood. She'd forgotten just how idyllic the garden was. A spacious lawn, bordered by trees and wide flower beds, stretched way down to the bottom of the garden, where a silver birch tree stood. Hedging ran all the way around the perimeter, interrupted only by Mr Greenwood's workshop on one side, and the wooden gate to a small orchard on the other.

The lawn was split in half by a path of large round flat stones, which carried on down the garden, past an ancient sundial, a stone birdbath and a sturdy wooden bird table. Halfway along, two other stone paths led off to the sides – one to the orchard, the other to Mr Greenwood's workshop.

Despite it being the middle of winter, there was no shortage of colour in the Greenwoods' garden. Around the perimeter, were greens of every shade and hue, from holly bushes, conifers and camellias, to cotoneasters, ferns, laurels and bay trees. Here and there, dogwood branches gave a burst of bright red, alongside the yellow blooms of mahonias. Deep oranges and crimsons were supplied by witch hazels, whilst the winter sunshine brought out an enchanting, sweet fragrance from the bright yellow chimonanthus.

Betty breathed in the perfume and surveyed the scene before her. There was beauty as far as the eye could see. Looking over the top of the hedge, she could see the meadows, pastures and fields, leading right up to Lundy Woods in the distance. It was perfect.

A little gingerly, without the reassurance of her stick, Betty walked along the path to the bottom of the garden, where the tall silver birch was located. The area around the foot of the tree resembled a fairy garden, for it had in the middle, a miniature white marble statuette of a maiden, sitting on a rock, holding a long staff. She was surrounded by four other small white figures in different poses.

Betty stared at the maiden in the middle. She had often admired her. The slim, graceful figure had fine delicate features, beneath long tresses of hair. A crown of tiny stars encircled her head, giving her the appearance of a queen. The white stone from which she was carved gave her a cold exquisite beauty. There was something about her today which held Betty's gaze and made her want to linger.

In fact, the more Betty looked at the statuette, the more she seemed to fancy that it glowed a little at the edges. She rubbed her eyes and looked again. Perhaps she was mistaken, but she had that strange sensation from before: that feeling of happiness, of sunshine, of green fields and of Harry.

Betty was so deep in thought that she didn't hear Mr Greenwood emerging from his workshop until he was right beside her, and the small Pomeranian was barking with pleasure to see him again.

John tickled the ear of the little dog, and explained to Betty that he'd managed to straighten out the walking stick, and made good many of the scratches and gouges. It had had a coat of varnish but now needed time to dry. If he gave her a lift home, could she manage without it till later in the evening?

Betty saw her opportunity. She had made a clear decision in her head, and was now about to seize the chance to make things happen. She invited Mr Greenwood and his children to join her for supper at the cottage. She would be making a big pot of stew. Would they care to come along and share it as a thank you?

Mr Greenwood grinned. The invitation was gratefully accepted, for Betty's reputation as a cook was well known throughout the village. Her cuisine was based on the wild ingredients she regularly foraged for in the local fields and woods, using her expert knowledge of plants and herbs. She favoured traditional recipes but with her own unique twist. The results were always delicious, and no one ever declined an invitation to dine with her.

Soon, Betty was back with John Greenwood in the truck, heading for home, her head full of plans. In her mind's eye, she could see the guinea pigs happily nibbling grass in that wonderful garden. She had found their new home – of that, she was sure.

Back in the Greenwoods' garden, the sun continued to smile down upon the lawn, and a slight breeze played amongst the leaves of the evergreens.

The bare branches of the silver birch tree rustled gently around its elegant silver trunk. Beneath, in its patterned shade, the ring of five marble statuettes had a distinct glow, particularly the figure at its centre.

Upon the beautiful stone lips of the white marble maiden, appeared a tiny smile.

Chapter 5

The Love Potion

THE guinea pigs were overjoyed when Betty added big handfuls of fresh sweet meadow hay into their box. They dived into it; they played in it; they stuck their noses into it and threw it over their heads. Finally, they settled down contentedly to munch on it.

Their box was now actually four boxes joined together. Each piggy had plenty of room to settle down and relax in their own space.

More joy was to come later that afternoon when Betty let them out for their daily run.

This time, she sprinkled pieces of the new dried food around the carpet for their treasure hunt – not too much – for their tiny stomachs had got to get used to it.

It was still a massive treat. Alfie and Little Rufus tore around at top speed, gobbling up the tasty dried seeds and flakes, each desperate to stop the other one from getting more than their fair share. In contrast, Hazel and Piggy Mama both took their time, savouring each delicious mouthful, and crunching away, with their eyes half closed, each time they found a tasty new morsel.

It was like the proper Christmas Day they had never had.

Betty watched their obvious joy, delightedly. They were happy now, but little did they know what greater happiness she had in store for them. If her plan worked out, they were going to have the best home ever, with a wonderful family. They'd be well loved, well looked after – and far away from the Brays.

After the piggies had (eventually) been rounded up, and placed back in their extended box, Betty got to work preparing for her visitors. She cooked, she tidied, she dusted, and she waited, desperately hoping that the evening would turn out the way that she wanted.

By evening, the stew was bubbling away in the pot, and a golden-topped rhubarb crumble was just coming out of the oven, when a knock sounded at the front door.

"Fingers crossed, my dears!" Betty whispered to the piggies as she left the kitchen and went to greet her guests. Betty turned the handle and opened the door.

On the step, was Mrs Bray.

With her was another young woman. Both had their arms folded, but their expressions differed considerably. Mrs Bray looked as if she wanted to turn heel and run. The other woman, standing defensively in front of her, had a mean determined look. She didn't bother with pleasantries.

"I am here to get back what *you* have stolen!" she snapped.

Betty opened her mouth to speak, but the woman didn't give her a chance, "And don't even *think* of trying to frighten *me* with feathers and funny lights. You're no witch. *I* don't believe in any of that magic rubbish!"

Yet again, Betty was in a position where she had to think fast. She gave the clock in the hall a furtive glance. She had around six minutes before the Greenwoods were due to arrive.

"Oh dear," she replied, sounding totally heartbroken, "I'm so sorry to hear that – especially tonight of all nights."

"Eh?" responded the woman, rather taken aback at the strange response.

Betty had noticed that she wore a necklace with the name 'Rowena' on it. She remembered a conversation she'd had with Ernie Bostock, in his hardware store, that very morning.

He'd told her a juicy bit of gossip about a girl named

Rowena, a cousin of Mr Bray's, from the next village. She was a bit of a pushy madam, by all accounts, who'd decided she wanted to marry before the year was out. She was measuring up all the local men with decent-sized houses. Apparently, she'd set her sights on John Greenwood.

Betty continued to shake her head sadly, "To think my most special love potion will go to waste."

"Your what?" asked the woman, sharply.

"My special love potion, "replied Betty. "I felt the strongest urge to prepare one for tonight." She kept a careful eye on the woman's face, noting her reactions. 'Rowena' had latched onto the word 'love', and was listening intently.

Her face fell as Betty waved her hand and added, "It's okay though, to someone like you, this will just sound ridiculous."

"What will?" asked Rowena, who'd clearly forgotten all her indignation on behalf of Mrs Bray (who was standing, ignored, behind her).

Betty continued in a soft voice, "I had one of my dreams last night, you see. I was standing by the most beautiful *rowan* tree..."

She definitely had the woman's attention now.

"A rowan is a tree of both magic and wisdom," Betty told her. "It gave me a sign that True Love's bond would be formed this very night."

Rowena tried to scoff, but it was

rather half-hearted, and the noise came out more like a small cough. She continued to stare at Betty, her eyes silently imploring her to say more.

Betty continued, "It told me that a beautiful young maiden would cross my path before the night was out. I was to have a special potion ready to seal Love's knot, and secure blessed happiness for this maiden and her choice of husband."

Rowena's expression had now softened slightly, and all the meanness had left her face. She looked more wistful and girlish.

Betty reached out a soft hand and rested it gently on one of Rowena's. "Feel free to walk away. You don't need to listen to an old fool like me..."

Rowena's eyes seemed to brim with tears. As Betty began to pull back her hand, Rowena grabbed it to detain her. Betty feigned surprise. "Was I wrong? Would you... like to give it a try?"

Rowena bit her bottom lip, and silently nodded her head. Betty asked in a sympathetic tone, "Do you want to wait here while I fetch it?"

"Yes please," Rowena whispered. She remained fixed to the spot as Betty turned and went down the hallway to her kitchen.

She almost felt sorry for the girl, but she reminded herself that the piggies' future was at stake, and this was a relative of the Brays. She headed for the jug of stock – a concoction of red wine, herbs and spices – left over from creating the stew. She poured some into an old-fashioned goblet that she kept on the shelf.

Carefully, Betty carried it back down the hallway to where Rowena waited, expectantly. (It had all been too much for Mrs Bray who had seized her opportunity to escape back to the safety of her own home.)

Betty held the goblet between her hands as if it was a priceless treasure, and 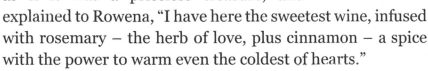 explained to Rowena, "I have here the sweetest wine, infused with rosemary – the herb of love, plus cinnamon – a spice with the power to warm even the coldest of hearts."

She had glanced at the clock on the way back, praying that time was on her side. She offered the goblet slowly, and Rowena duly accepted it with great reverence.

"Think of your true love and drink deeply," Betty urged in a quiet voice, as if confiding the greatest secret of all time.

Rowena closed her eyes for a moment and then lifted the goblet to her lips. She drained the cup dry and gaped at the empty receptacle, waiting for something dramatic to happen.

It didn't. There was silence.

Rowena looked at Betty. Betty looked back.

Betty was about to speak when the sound of voices on the street interrupted the silence. Rowena turned around to look. Her eyes nearly popped out of her head when she saw John Greenwood himself walking towards them, with Billy and Molly at his side.

From behind Rowena's back, Betty was able to wave frantically at Mr Greenwood, pressing her finger to her lips, and giving him a pantomime wink. She greeted him loudly in an astonished tone, "Why, John, whatever brings you here?"

Mr Greenwood paused, trying to work out what was going on.

Betty continued, "I haven't seen you in *ages*. What brings you here of all places?"

"Why Betty," he replied, instinctively playing along. "Do you know, we were just passing, and I got the urge to call in and say hello."

His children looked baffled as he carried on politely, "Is this a convenient time or shall we call again another day?" He waited for Betty's reply, slightly unnerved by the young woman staring at him so intently.

"Not at all," said Betty quickly. "This young lady – sorry, I don't know your name, dear," she pretended. She looked at Rowena with a concerned smile, but received no coherent response.

"This young lady was just on her way to visit next door when she felt a little faint, so I was giving her a drink of water," Betty explained.

She directed her attention to Rowena, "Has the *drink* helped you at all, my dear?"

Rowena nodded, a simpering smile spreading across her face, accompanied by a slight blush on her cheeks.

"Let me assist you," said Betty, taking Rowena gently by the arm, and guiding her down the short path. Betty carried on leading her round to the Bray's front door, which she opened, and gently but firmly pushed her inside.

Rowena stood looking out at John Greenwood, grinning foolishly from ear to ear. Betty whispered to her, "The potion will work its magic from this moment, my dear. The knot has been tied, but do *not* let your true love set eyes upon you for a second time before the next Full Moon, or the knot will unravel." She then pulled the Brays' door shut, leaving the stupefied Rowena inside.

Betty returned to her own doorway, beckoning urgently to John and his two children to make their way into her cottage. Mr Greenwood led the way, whilst Billy and Molly, as puzzled as ever, headed up the steps after their father.

Once inside the door, Betty ushered them into the kitchen before giving in to a fit of giggles. The Greenwoods couldn't help giggling too, as they waited for an explanation of her eccentric behaviour.

Controlling her amusement, Betty promised all would be revealed over supper. In the meantime, whilst she dished up the food, would they like to meet her furry little house guests?

The Greenwoods were more than surprised to see four little guinea pigs sitting there, amongst piles of hay, in a large extended cardboard box, on the floor of Betty's kitchen.

And so, the Greenwoods were introduced to Hazel, Alfie,

Little Rufus and Piggy Mama. The piggies were stroked, tickled and admired.

So far so good, thought Betty.

Soon her guests were sitting comfortably around her large oak kitchen table. The cheerful crackling of the wood fire added to the relaxed atmosphere. Wonderful aromas filled the kitchen, from both Betty's stew bubbling on the stove and the many bundles of dried herbs and flowers hanging from the surrounding walls.

As expected, Betty served up a sumptuous feast. The rich flavours of chestnut and wild mushroom stew were accompanied by Betty's refreshing elderflower cordial. A mouth-watering dessert of rhubarb crumble, sweetened with cicely leaves, followed. The meal was rounded off with tasty chicory coffee, and creamy cashew nut cheese complemented by tangy rowanberry and crab apple jelly. Everyone thoroughly enjoyed it – even Molly.

Despite arriving in rather a bad mood, she had begun to relax and smile as the meal had progressed. She had totally forgotten that she was supposed to be a moody teenager, a role she had been practising for the past year of her life.

Molly had accompanied her father and brother to Betty's house under protest. The threat of having to feed herself that night was the only argument which had finally won her over, especially as her father had said, yes, it was perfectly fine for her to contact the takeaway in the neighbouring town – so long as she funded it herself. She had sullenly given in, ready to suffer her way through the evening like a true martyr.

However, along with John and Billy, she had listened intently during the meal, as Betty recounted the events of Christmas Day. Like them, she was horrified at the treatment of the little guinea pigs at the hands of the Brays.

Billy piped up that he was not at all surprised. He knew the Bray twins only too well from school. They were always playing nasty tricks on other kids, and had even once buried Mrs Kinder's car keys under the school geraniums.

They listened in awe as Betty described the woodland animals storming into number 12. They laughed heartily as she recalled her confrontation with Mr Bray, especially the part where she had sent him scuttling home with her 'magic' yellow feather. Tonight's events with Rowena they found especially amusing.

"Make sure she sets eyes on you again before that Full Moon, Dad," laughed Molly, "or you'll never be free of her!"

By the time the meal had finished, Betty had told the Greenwoods everything – everything that is, except for the part about the silver orb. For some reason she could not explain, Betty held back on that. It felt too precious, too personal to share at present, and she was still working out in her mind what it truly was. She merely said she had looked into the garden of number 12 on an impulse.

As her guests sat back in their chairs, too full to eat another mouthful, Betty knew it was her moment to speak plainly. She swallowed, and was just plucking up the courage to ask the question she had been working up to all night – when Billy suddenly spoke. "Betty, guinea pigs like to run around a garden and eat grass."

He spoke with the direct honesty that children so often use when they say what's on their mind. He didn't know how to dress it up like an adult would.

"They need a minimum space of seven square feet..." he carried on, from his expert knowledge of animals.

"Billy..." his father started to say, but Betty stopped him.

"It's okay, John, Billy has a point. That's why I need to find them a new home. Much as I love them, I know they could never be safe in my garden."

"We could have them!" Billy exclaimed. He looked at his father with pleading eyes.

John Greenwood smiled at his son and then looked at Betty. "What do you think, Betty?"

Betty looked around the table at each of the Greenwoods' faces, and replied happily, "I think that would be perfect."

Outside the window of number 14, in the cold darkness of the winter's night, a silver orb shone brightly. As it floated, gently twinkling in the murky air, four other small round coloured lights danced merrily around it, as if in celebration.

Chapter 6

Madam Pom and the Tomcat

THERE were ten days left before the next Full Moon appeared in the night sky, and Molly Greenwood had a mission – to ensure that her father bumped into Rowena Bray at every opportunity.

They met her coming out of shops, walking through the village, even driving along the road. Molly took no chances. Poor Rowena's face became a picture of greater misery and disappointment each time she laid eyes on Mr Greenwood.

Finally, they met her by complete chance in the grocery shop, where Rowena was just adding a bottle of red wine to the basket she was carrying – it contained jars of cinnamon sticks and dried rosemary.

Meanwhile, it was agreed that the guinea pigs would spend the rest of the cold winter months with Betty. Once spring came, along with the better weather, they would go to their new home, where they could enjoy the freedom of a pleasant garden. Most important of all – they would be safely far away from the Brays.

During their remaining time together, Betty and Hazel had become ever closer. Each night, whilst Alfie, Little Rufus and Mama slept, Betty continued to sit by the fireside with

Hazel on her lap. Recently, she had taken to stroking the little piggy with a soft clean shoe brush, as she talked to her in a low gentle voice. Little did Betty know that Hazel actually listened to every word she said.

For Hazel had a skill which set her apart from other guinea pigs – she could understand most human speech. She had inherited this ability from an ancestor, way back in her mother's bloodline.

This ancestor was named Grama Lizzy. She was a wise old guinea pig who had lived many, many, many ages ago. Although some of her wisdom and knowledge had been passed down through the generations, her ability to understand human speech had not – until that is, Hazel was born. Alfie, Mama and Little Rufus could pick out occasional words and phrases, but none of them shared Hazel's much fuller understanding.

On this particular night, as they sat together in the rocking chair, Hazel was worried – very, very worried indeed. On the night when the Greenwoods came for supper, she was sure that she had heard something about the piggies going to a new home. Nothing had been said within her hearing since, and she had very much hoped that she had been mistaken.

However, at this moment, Hazel was picking up an intense feeling of sadness from Betty. Whilst snuggled on her knee, Hazel had given Betty's hand a little lick of reassurance. Betty had smiled down at the guinea pig, tickled her ear and said softly, "How I will miss you, my dear."

Hazel had frozen. She felt puzzled and frightened. She had been right all along – they were going to leave Betty, but why?

Betty continued, "I know it's for the best. You will have a beautiful sunny garden to run around in, far away from those horrid young boys and their even worse father."

Now Hazel understood. Of course, the piggies were terrified of The Horrid Loud One and his boys, but the thought of leaving the loving home they had with Betty was deeply upsetting. Miserably, Hazel lay flat and tried to focus on the soothing feeling of the soft brush running through her fur.

The wheel of the year was slowly turning. The days were becoming longer, and spring was in the air. The snowdrops had led the way, pushing their sharp green tips through the cold hard soil. Soon, the celandines had joined them, the daffodils, the crocuses and the primroses too, their sweet nectar tempting the first bumble bees from their winter hibernation.

For once, the early signs of the new season were of little cheer to Betty. She was up early, as always. It was the day she and the Greenwoods had been planning for, the day when she knew the Brays would be out, and the day when she was to say goodbye to the piggies.

She spoke brightly to them, trying to convince herself that she was not going to miss the small furry creatures who had become such a big part of her life.

"You will love the garden," Betty told them, "and the Greenwoods are such kind people. They will look after you so much better than those dreadful people at number 12."

Hazel had explained what was happening to the rest of her family, and they now sat rather subdued, wondering what the day would bring.

All too soon for Betty, the sound of a truck could be heard, pulling up outside. Moments later, Billy and his father were on the doorstep, with a large deep box in Mr Greenwood's hands. It was just a plain box, as they had no wish to broadcast the fact that they were collecting the piggies just in case word got back to number 12.

Betty welcomed them in. "I've got everything ready," she said, forcing a smile. She led them through to the kitchen and gestured for John to place the box on the kitchen table.

Betty had some hay ready, which she'd taken from the guinea pigs' house that morning. She now spread it inside the big plain box on the table. That way, they'd have a familiar scent to keep them calm on their journey.

Knowing it was always bad to prolong a painful moment, Betty immediately got on with the business of transferring the guinea pigs. As she lifted each one into the box, she planted a small kiss on the silky head.

She left Hazel till last, "Goodbye, my special one," she said, before giving her a kiss, which lasted just that little bit longer.

Inside the box, the four piggies' hearts were beating fast. It might not be a bad thing that was happening, but it was strange and new. More than anything, they did not want to leave Betty. They had become used to her gentle voice, alongside the chin rubs and the ear tickles. Would they ever have those again?

"Goodbye, my dears," they heard her say.

"Don't worry, Betty, "said Mr Greenwood. "We promise we will take good care of them – won't we, Billy?"

"Definitely!" said Billy, beaming with joy at their new pets.

"Come for afternoon tea, tomorrow," added Mr Greenwood, "See how they've settled in. I'll come for you at one."

"Thank you, that would be lovely," said Betty brightening up, "I'll bring a cake!"

The piggies could not help but tremble slightly, as their new box was lifted up, carried out of the kitchen into the fresh air, and loaded into the truck, outside.

Upon arrival at Bowood, the piggies were taken straight into an outhouse, attached to the kitchen. A latched door led into the cosy little room.

They were to be kept indoors, safe from predators, and from extremes of temperature. The room was warm in winter, but cool in summer. It would be calm and quiet too.

Awaiting them in the outhouse, was the fine sturdy hutch that Mr Greenwood had made especially for them, from the best pine wood. It stood against an inside wall, on thick legs, around twelve inches from the floor.

It had two levels, with a separate door for each one. The doors both had a large mesh front so the piggies would be able to see out. Inside, it was spacious and roomy.

On each level, there was a cosy enclosed nesting box, with a piggy-sized hole for an entrance. In addition, there was a wooden igloo on each floor, allowing each piggy to have a quiet place of their own when they needed it.

In the corner of the lower level, an entrance led to a long wooden ramp with regular footholds. This in turn led down to a large wooden-framed, mesh-sided run on the workshop floor, so the piggies could stretch their legs whenever they wished. It had its own separate floor of wood to keep their feet from harm.

When the guinea pigs were lifted into the hutch, it felt like piggy paradise. It was lined with fresh newspaper, and topped with soft wood shavings, followed by lots and lots of sweet meadow hay. On each floor, a water bottle hung at just the right level for a piggy's mouth, along with a nice big bowl of dried food.

They were now left in peace to explore the hutch. The hay with the familiar scent had been placed in and spread around. It now provided great reassurance.

The piggies sniffed their way around their new home, loving it more and more as they did so. After some time, they were suddenly interrupted by an indignant voice.

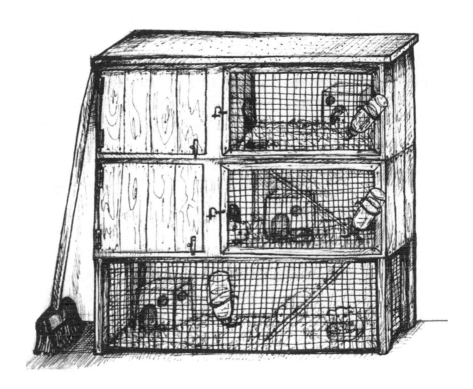

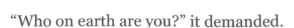

"Who on earth are you?" it demanded.

The piggies froze. A dog's face was staring at them through the wire mesh. They instinctively froze and stared back fearfully at this potential predator.

"I *asked* who you were," repeated the dog, impatiently.

Despite her initial panic, Hazel was rather annoyed by the dog's tone of voice. Mama had always insisted that they use their manners, at all times. Clearly, this dog had been brought up differently.

"*We* are Hazel, Alfie, Little Rufus and Mama," she replied. "Who might *you* be?"

"Well, if you want my full pedigree name, it is *Madam Pom Pom de Belvedere Dancing Queen,*" the dog announced proudly, "but I am known as Madam Pom for short."

Little Rufus giggled at this, before being shushed by Piggy Mama.

Madam Pom glared at him icily, before adding, "*I* am the highest-ranking pedigree Pomeranian of The National Kennel Association."

She was perplexed to see that the guinea pigs did not seem remotely impressed.

"What's a Pomeranian?" asked Alfie.

"It is a very sophisticated breed of dog," replied Madam airily. "What sort of creatures are you?"

"We are guinea pigs," Mama told her.

"And why, exactly, are you all here, in *my* home?" demanded Madam.

"Well, it seems to be our home now too," said Mama.

"Humph!" Madam Pom snorted, in disgust. "We'll see about that!"

She then turned tail and disappeared out of the door.

"Stupid *Poo*meranian!" said Little Rufus, as they watched her go.

"Rufus!" scolded Mama.

Outside in the Bowood garden, a large grey tabby cat, by the name of Bruce, was waiting on the roof of Mr Greenwood's workshop. He was the neighbourhood tough guy, a fierce looking creature with a mighty reputation. The birds lived in fear of him, as did the rats and the mice. He showed no mercy to any of his victims, or so he led all to believe. He told tall tales of savaging small creatures, far and wide. No one had ever witnessed this, but then no one ever waited around to find out.

One of Bruce's favourite pastimes was teasing Madam Pom. He loved to creep along, and appear, unexpectedly, somewhere in the garden of Bowood. It could be from up a tree, from behind a bush, on top of the workshop or simply under the gate. It really didn't matter how or where he appeared, as long as it annoyed Madam Pom – which it always did. The pedigree Pomeranian would be outraged and would chase around barking furiously until the feline intruder gleefully made his escape.

Bruce was now waiting patiently for today's entertainment to begin. He did not have long to wait, for Madam Pom came bursting out through the dog flap of the kitchen door, into the garden, in a total temper.

Bruce grinned to himself. Good! She was already looking annoyed. He wondered how quickly he could wind her up to boiling point today.

However, this time, when Madam Pom looked up and spotted him, she seemed to stop and think. This was not the reaction Bruce normally received, so he moved in closer. Still, Madam Pom simply gazed up at him, as if deep in thought.

As Bruce moved in even closer, the pedigree dog looked pleased, and said, "I've got something to discuss which might interest you."

For the first time ever, the tomcat and the Pomeranian dog suspended their hostilities and had a conversation. When Bruce padded away, he had a sly grin on his face, as did Madam Pom.

Chapter 7

Danger in the Night

THE piggies were now resting comfortably in their new hutch. Between them, they had explored every inch, and were now rather tired. Mama and Little Rufus were snoozing in the upstairs nesting box, whilst Hazel and Alfie sat two levels below, in the run under the hutch, munching on a pile of hay.

Hazel and her brother were a little surprised when Madam Pom reappeared through the kitchen door. They were even more surprised when she came close and lay down to whisper to them in a kindly tone, "Hello again. How are you settling in?"

"Very nicely, thank you," Hazel whispered back a little cautiously, exchanging puzzled glances with Alfie.

"Has anyone shown you the garden yet?" asked Madam Pom.

At this, Hazel immediately perked up, "The garden?"

"Yes," replied Madam Pom, "would you like to see it?"

"Hazel..." began Alfie, but his sister was not listening.

"Yes! We would!" Hazel exclaimed, barely able to contain her excitement.

"Good, none of the family knows it," replied Madam Pom,

"but there is a hole in the corner of the wall, behind the cupboard."

"It leads out into the garden, but is hidden from view by a leafy evergreen bush growing in front of the wall. It's far too small for me, but it would be fine for you."

The eager look on Hazel's face said it all. Madam Pom knew she had achieved what she wanted. "I'll be back tonight, when it's dark," she whispered. "Be ready!"

Alfie looked at his sister, in horror, "Hazel, Mama will never let..."

"She won't know!" interrupted Hazel.

Poor Alfie. He knew Mama would be furious with them both, but he could not let his headstrong sister go alone.

Once the Greenwoods had retired to bed, and the Moon was in the sky, Madam Pom returned. Hazel and Alfie were waiting for her down in the run, having slipped out quietly, without Mama suspecting.

Madam had used her teeth to pull up part of the wire mesh, which formed the side of the run. She had chosen a spot in the corner, near the wall, where it was hard to see. This separated it from the wooden frame and created a gap just wide enough for a guinea pig to slip through.

Once Hazel and Alfie had squeezed out, she showed them

to the hole behind the wooden
cupboard. She explained how
they should pass through this to
the other side, where a camellia
bush grew. If they pushed past
this, they would find themselves in
the garden. She'd go through her dog
flap and meet them out there.

Hazel led the way, with Alfie reluctantly
following close after. Once behind the bush, they each
pushed out into the garden.

Here, they stopped to gaze ahead at the huge wide-open
space around them. The Moon was full, providing ample
light to see by, yet still the plants, trees and bushes around
the edges were full of dark shadows. Where was Madam
Pom? She should have been here by now.

Impatient as ever, Hazel decided not to wait. Before Alfie
could stop her, she had begun walking down the lawn
to explore.

Alfie was terrified. Who knew what predators could be out
there? His fear, and the strange unfamiliar smells in the
chilly night air, made him shiver.

"Hazel!" he called after her, nervously. "We should wait
for Madam Pom." Where had that dog got to?

Hazel wasn't listening. All she could smell in the air was
freedom.

She shut her eyes and breathed in deeply. She was

exhilarated by the huge space which, to her eyes, seemed to go on forever. There were no walls of any description to confine her or imprison her. This was the feeling she'd been yearning for, for so long.

As Alfie watched her in alarm, a little voice sounded beside him. It was a wood mouse, looking at him with concern in her eyes. "Haven't you heard that Bruce the cat prowls at night?"

She was scurrying home to feed her children and had only stopped to warn these new strangers of the risk they were taking. She now hurried on her way.

That was enough for Alfie, "Hazel!" he wheeked. "Let's go back in!"

His words went unheard, for Hazel was now halfway down the garden. Alfie watched her helplessly, wondering if he should simply forget Madam Pom and follow her.

But then he noticed something.

This something was dark, and large, and was moving very slowly and purposefully.

This something was Bruce, the cat.

He was prowling slowly but surely across the lawn – towards Hazel. She was oblivious, too full of thoughts of freedom and exploration to notice.

Alfie gasped. He felt pure terror, and wanted to run for his life, but his sister was alone on the lawn, with a cat about to pounce on her. He took a deep breath, swallowed his fears, and ran as hard as he could towards the stalking cat.

His sudden movement caught Bruce's eye, and he stopped in his tracks, shocked to see a guinea pig hurtling towards him at top speed. He was even more astonished when the guinea pig bowled straight into his back legs, knocking his balance away, and sending him sprawling.

But not for long. He soon sprang back up onto his feet.

"Run, Hazel!" Alfie wheeked at the top of his voice.

Hazel awoke from her dreaming to see a cat, standing over Alfie and hissing angrily, whilst her brother looked up at him in terror.

"Alfie!" she shrieked. She ran towards the cat and sank her teeth into his front paw, causing him to leap up into the air, screeching in pain.

Bruce was now beyond angry. His mouth was open wide, baring his sharp teeth, as he snarled and hissed at his attackers. He lunged forward and pinned Hazel to the ground.

Hazel shut her eyes tightly, hoping the pain would be over with quickly. She thought she was about to breathe her last when...

"Halt!" ordered a voice.

The voice seemed to come from nowhere, yet its impact was immediate. Bruce froze.

Hazel opened her eyes, and saw, to her huge relief, the silver orb of light from Christmas Day. It had saved her life before, and now it seemed to be back, to do so again.

It was hovering over the head of Bruce, the tomcat,

81

stealing his attention entirely away from the guinea pig beneath him. In addition, four coloured lights encircled his head. He was now staring at the lights without blinking, a look of dread upon his face.

The voice had spoken only once, yet its power remained in the silence. It had been a high silvery voice which echoed around the garden. It was a voice which clearly expected to be obeyed.

It spoke again, "I summon each of you to appear before me, immediately."

Hazel scrambled to her feet, as Bruce's paws fell from her body, and Alfie raced to her side.

"Follow!" commanded the voice, as the silver orb, and the other lights, began to lead the way, down the garden.

The tomcat did as he was told, obediently trailing after the lights. The two guinea pigs followed on behind.

The animals travelled in total silence, none of them knowing what to expect. The walk felt like the longest walk of their lives.

Right down the garden they were led – way down to the very bottom, where a silver birch tree stood.

The truth of the mysterious silver light was about to be revealed.

Chapter 8

A Lesson Learnt

BENEATH the silver birch tree, at the bottom of the Greenwoods' garden, the floating orbs of light came to a standstill. So did Hazel, Alfie and Bruce, the tomcat. All stared in awe and wonder at the sight before them.

The five orbs now hovered over five white marble statuettes, at the foot of the tree. In the moonlit night, the eyes of the nervous animals were naturally drawn to the majestic maiden in the centre, who sat on a stone, higher and more prominent than the others.

As the animals watched, the largest of the silver orbs floated above the maiden. It then descended, and seemed to expand around her to form a silvery silhouette of light.

As it did so, the marble figure began to lose her stony white appearance, and slowly, but surely, gained colour and movement, setting her apart from the other statuettes, which remained solid and still.

The statuette was now a live tall slender maiden, with delicate pale features. Her long straight hair became silky shiny tresses of the whitest blonde, whilst her eyes turned to an icy blue, beneath her pale lids. Her lips softened, taking on a silvery-blue tinge.

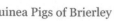

Around her head, sat a crown of luminous stars. Her long gown, of the palest shimmering blue, followed the contours of her figure closely until it reached her feet, and draped over a pair of silver slippers. A sparkling cord of tiny stars encircled her waist, and hung loosely at her side. Her hand rested on a long slim staff, topped with a large round moonstone.

Around her, the other four orbs of light, still floated in the air.

Once the transformation was complete, the icy blue eyes gazed upon Hazel, Alfie and Bruce, who trembled with fear, as they looked back.

They heard the same high silvery voice, light as air, yet full of unspoken power.

"You find yourselves in the presence of the Moon Queen,"

she announced, "and your fear is to be expected."

Her face was calm, yet her anger could be felt. The moonstone atop of her staff appeared to glow sharply, as if to reflect that anger.

"The cat will stay before me. The other creatures will stand apart," she continued.

"I will speak with the cat, but not until the others, who should be here, are present."

She nodded her head slightly, and addressed the four orbs of light, "Sprites!"

The first of the four lights moved to hang in the air over Hazel and Alfie, before leading them a little distance away from the Moon Queen. The other three lights drifted away up the garden, towards the house.

Within moments, they could be seen returning, one leading Madam Pom down the garden, the other two guiding Mama and Little Rufus, close behind.

Upon their arrival at the bottom of the garden, Mama and Little Rufus were led over to join Hazel and Alfie. They looked startled and confused but there was no time to speak or ask questions. They sat quietly, trying to make sense of the scene before them.

The comforting presence of Mama was welcome to Hazel and Alfie. They moved to sit closely by her side.

There was no similar comfort for Madam Pom. She was taken to sit by Bruce, under the fierce gaze of the Moon Queen. There they both sat with their heads bowed.

The four coloured orbs of light now hovered by the Moon Queen once more, each above a marble statuette. Just as she had been transformed to life, the same process began for the other four stony figures. Each orb moved down to form a silhouette around one of the statues, gradually melting away its solid marble appearance, and bringing it colour and movement.

To the Moon Queen's right, there now sat a mermaid on a rock, who carried an open clam shell in her lap. Long wavy tresses of golden hair framed her warm friendly face and cascaded over her full curvaceous figure. A twinkle of merriment seemed to play around her eyes and lips.

Next to her, sat a slight boyish figure, on a toadstool, with delicate transparent wings upon his back. His face was elf-like beneath his wavy hair. He held a reed pipe to his lips, as if ready to play a light airy melody.

On the Moon Queen's left, was a young man, of muscular build, with a close brown beard and a dusky complexion. He held a spade between his large hands, and stood poised as if he was about to dig deep into the earth.

Alongside him, was a girl with a shock of bright red hair which resembled a flame, as it swirled into a single point at the crown of her head. Her sharp green eyes were cat-like, and the expression on her face hinted she could be quick to anger. She sat upon a stone with a lantern in her hand.

Madam Pom and Bruce had been mesmerised by the sight of the sprites transforming before their eyes, and had momentarily forgotten their fear. However, it now returned, as the two sorry animals sat with their heads bowed, quivering.

The Moon Queen looked coldly upon them. "You have done wrong here tonight, in my garden. The creatures you sought to harm were brought here by me, to live under my protection."

Bruce and Madam Pom stared nervously at the ground as she spoke.

"Before you feel the force of my anger," the Moon Queen said, "you may speak, and explain your actions."

At this point, the unfortunate cat and dog raised their heads, and dared to look directly at the queen they so feared. The whole story came tumbling out. It had been a plan, created by Madam Pom. There had been no intention to harm the guinea pigs in any way; the aim was merely to frighten them. The hope was that they would think again about wanting to live at Bowood.

"I wanted them to run away, and live somewhere else," explained Madam Pom, in a faltering voice.

Bruce, the tomcat, admitted that he had agreed to frighten them, in order to strengthen his fearsome reputation with the other creatures.

Both cat and dog now bowed their heads even lower, and said how deeply sorry they were.

There was a frosty silence as the Moon Queen stared at their heads, hanging low before her.

"Hear this now, and mark my words. This garden is my kingdom, and all creatures within it must obey my rule of law. You will now feel my displeasure and pay for your actions."

"Sprites!" she continued, "You know what must be done."

Oro, the winged boy, was the first to move. He was a sprite of the air, as the dog and cat were about to find out. With his wings fluttering, he rose up above them, and pointed both hands in their direction.

As he did so, a strong wind blasted around the dog and cat, flattening their fur to their bodies, and whipping up earth, twigs and leaves in a harsh whirlwind of air about them. The dog and the cat both squeezed their eyes shut, curling up to protect themselves, and huddling tightly together.

Moments later, as quickly as it had started, the wind dropped. It took a few seconds for Madam Pom and Bruce to risk opening their eyes once more, before looking at each other with startled faces.

Now up stepped Godfrig, the muscular earth sprite. He raised a hand, and pointed to the earth around the cat and the dog's feet.

The next thing they knew, the ground was trembling all around them, as if an earthquake was erupting beneath them. Poor Madam Pom and Bruce huddled yet closer together to withstand this latest torment.

With a deep rumble, the ground beneath them began to rise up into a high mound, with the cat and dog perched on top. They were kept there for a few dizzying moments, until the mound subsided with another rumble. When the earth finally settled, and the luckless animals were brought back down, they were both panting and trembling. A sorrier sight they could not have been.

Yet their ordeal was far from over, for now it was the turn of Fion, the fire sprite. Her green eyes glinted as she gazed intently at the two animals before her. Her flame red hair seemed to glow as she pointed with her finger, and drew a circle around the cat and the dog. Immediately, a ring of low

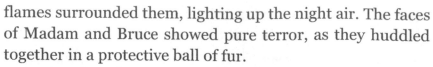

flames surrounded them, lighting up the night air. The faces of Madam and Bruce showed pure terror, as they huddled together in a protective ball of fur.

Seeing their fear, Merriel, the water sprite, leapt forward to take her turn. Despite having a tail, the mermaid could still move across the ground quickly on the points of her fins. She lifted her clam shell, and dowsed the flames with cooling water, much to the relief of Bruce and Madam Pom.

Fion, the fire sprite, was less than pleased. She glared at her, with furious green eyes, exclaiming, "Merriel, you know you were supposed to soak the creatures!"

"I think they have learnt their lesson," replied Merriel firmly, glancing at the dog and cat with compassion in her eyes.

Madam Pom and Bruce were now a sad sight, with their fur ruffled, matted, and full of bits of debris. The expressions on their faces told a sorry tale.

The Moon Queen looked down at them, as they now sat wearily before her. "Let that be a lesson for you both on how it feels to fear for your lives."

She pointed with her staff. "Go now, and remember my words!" she commanded.

"Yes, Your Majesty," both animals mumbled together, before taking their leave.

Bruce stumbled across the garden, scrambled up a tree, and tore off into the darkness. Madam Pom then trotted off, as quickly as her ruined dignity and tired body would allow, back up the garden, and in through her dog flap in the kitchen door.

Hazel, Alfie, Mama and Little Rufus had watched the scene unfolding before their eyes, in complete amazement. They stared, still silent, as the sprites now returned to their positions, by the Moon Queen.

Her Majesty's attention now returned to the guinea pigs. She beckoned to them to come closer, and sit at her feet, which they obediently did.

"Well, my little creatures, you heard me say that it was I who brought you here. The humans played their part, but little did they realise, it was under my direction."

The expression on the Moon Queen's face remained calm and icy, but her voice now sounded gentle and kind. The moonstone on the end of her staff had taken on a softer glow.

"You also heard me say that you are under my protection, and within the walls of this garden, that is so."

The four guinea pigs gazed up at the silvery figure above them, still almost too dazed to truly comprehend what she was saying.

It was finally Piggy Mama who found her voice, "Your Majesty, we are forever in your debt. You have saved the lives of myself and my children. We are most grateful – but may I dare to ask why we were chosen?"

The Moon Queen's blue eyes looked down at the four small creatures before her, a slight smile upon her lips. "Why, you have your first born to thank," she replied.

"Hazel?" asked Mama in astonishment.

The astonishment was felt even more keenly by Hazel herself. Her heart fluttered at the sound of her name.

"Indeed," continued the Moon Queen, "for she placed a Moon Wish."

Hazel's throat tightened, leaving her unable to speak, so it fell to her mother to respond, "A Moon Wish, Your Majesty?"

"Yes," said the Moon Queen, turning her attention directly to Hazel herself, "You may remember, Hazel, you placed a heartfelt wish at the time of the New Moon. You wished for a new life for yourself and your family. When the Full Moon came, your wish was granted."

The Moon Queen paused to let her words sink in. As she spoke, Hazel felt a strange sensation in her stomach. Her mind began racing. She had wished to the moon so often – one wish may well have fallen on a New Moon. Could it be that one of those wishes had actually worked? *Surely not.*

"The Moon actually listened to *me*?" she asked, timidly.

The strange sensation in Hazel's stomach grew stronger, as she beheld the silver blue eyes of the Moon Queen.

"Why not you, Hazel?" said the Moon Queen simply. "Anyone can make a New Moon Wish, and you did just that. You made it with all your heart, so much so that our Lady in the Sky listened to you."

The Moon Queen smiled, "You are no ordinary animal now, Hazel. You have been blessed by the Moon. That makes you incredibly special."

Hazel gasped. Her mouth went dry. She could barely take in what the Moon Queen was saying.

"Not only has your Moon Wish been fulfilled," said the Moon Queen, "but life has much more in store for you yet."

Hazel's heart thumped in her chest. Wild thoughts exploded in her mind. Those strange wild yearnings she had always felt, but never dared share with anyone, now seemed less hopeless. Her mind began bursting with questions, which she couldn't find the power to express.

There was total silence as the four guinea pigs sat before the Moon Queen, lost for words, trying hard to absorb the startling news. Alfie and Little Rufus gaped at Hazel, then at the Moon Queen, then at each other, as if they were dreaming.

The Moon Queen decided it was time to draw the night's events to a close. "There has been much to take in. You must each now go and seek rest. You may speak with me again, at the next Full Moon.

"However," she informed them, "this can only be between the hours of twilight and dawn. I am never seen by day's full light. "Should you need anything, my sprites: Godfrig, Merriel, Oro and Fion, will be on hand."

The Moon Queen spoke no more.

As the piggies looked on, the life faded quickly from the Moon Queen and her sprites. They each lost their colour, and reverted to their stony white marble appearances as garden statuettes, becoming still once again.

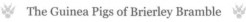

By the light of the bright moon, high up in the sky, the piggies huddled together for a few moments, taking comfort from each other. They each felt drained and exhausted, lacking the energy to even speak.

"Come along," Mama whispered. She glanced proudly at Hazel, and then began to lead the way. In silence, the four piggies travelled slowly back up the garden, each lost in their own thoughts.

As they neared the large camellia bush hiding the entrance back into the outhouse, Hazel hung back.

"Mama," she whispered, catching her mother's attention. "I will be in soon."

Her mother nodded, and led her other children to the leafy bush, which they slipped behind, disappearing from view.

Hazel stood on the grass, and lifted her face to gaze at the Full Moon. She closed her eyes, and breathed in the cool night air. The breeze caressed her ears, and played through her fur, as if to calm her mind after the night's drama. The strangest sensation now filled Hazel's body. Despite her exhaustion, she felt happier than she had ever felt in her whole life before. The big wide world was now truly opening up for one small curious guinea pig. She could taste freedom and adventure in the air, and feel it beneath her feet.

Without thinking, Hazel sat back on her haunches, and reached her face high to the Moon and stars. Her lithe body stretched out long and tall, as she threw back her head, and began to sing. Her song was like the chirping of a bird, sweet and high-pitched. It was a sound she didn't even know she could make, yet at this moment, it was her voice of deep-felt joy.

For how long she sang, she did not know. She just sang, and sang and sang.

Finally, a powerful sense of peace came over her, and she became still, quiet and calm.

With one last backwards glance at the Moon, Hazel headed for the leafy evergreen bush. She slipped behind it, and went in to join her family.

She would sleep with the sweetest contentment that night, knowing the future had endless possibilities.

Chapter 9
A Beautiful Sunny Garden

THE day dawned as a clear bright spring day. The sunlight streamed in through the windows of the outhouse, awaking the piggies from their deep slumber. They had each slept soundly in their new hutch, exhausted by the events of the night before. It was hard to believe that Bowood had been their home for less than twenty four hours.

Yet it was still strange to wake up somewhere new, without the comforting sound of Betty's cheerful voice. They waited quietly, on the top level of the hutch, nibbling on strands of hay, wondering if they would still get a tasty breakfast. Hazel, Alfie and Piggy Mama were rather too shy yet to call out for food as they had with Betty.

Little Rufus, however, had no such finer feelings. He wasn't going to risk starving again, as they had in the old hutch. He let out a full throated *wheeeek* at the top of his voice.

Within seconds, Billy Greenwood's tousled head appeared through the door from the kitchen. "Ah, piglets, you're awake!" He opened the hutch door, and gave each piggy a quick stroke.

He had been itching to come in and see them since he'd awoken that morning. Despite it being a Sunday, he'd been up since early light, desperate to see them again. He had been under strict instructions from his father to leave them in peace until they were ready.

"It will all still be strange and new for them," Mr Greenwood had warned his son.

Billy disappeared momentarily, but was soon back, with a plate of food in his hand. He had breakfast all ready, and it was quickly served: half a ripe juicy red strawberry for each piggy, alongside slivers of broccoli, cucumber and celery leaves.

Hazel, Alfie, Little Rufus and Piggy Mama were soon tucking in with gusto.

Billy saw to it that their water bottle was refreshed, and their bowl of dried food topped up. He added generous handfuls of meadow hay to each level of the hutch, and then left them to it.

"I've got to get things ready for you out in the garden!" he said excitedly before he left. Hazel's ears pricked up at the word 'garden'. Would they get to see the outside world in daylight today?

The piggies were soon full. They settled down comfortably to let their breakfast digest.

Alfie and Little Rufus began to tease Hazel, as brothers so love to do. Was *The Special One* okay this morning? Did *The Special One* enjoy her breakfast? Had *The Special One* any orders for them? Eventually, Piggy Mama had to intervene and put an end to it.

Hazel pointed out to them, rather huffily, that they were 'special' too, "You've got the Moon Queen's protection in the garden as well!"

Alfie and Little Rufus were happy to be reminded of this. "Just think what we can do now," said Alfie. "We can't get hurt, so when they let us out in the garden, we could have a go at climbing up…"

He was abruptly interrupted by his mother who had no wish to hear the end of that sentence. She pointed out that that was *not* what the Moon Queen had meant.

"She said you were protected from other animals. She did *not* mean you could do silly dangerous things!"

Alfie and his brother looked a little crestfallen at this. They'd have to rethink quite a few of their plans.

Later that morning, as the piggies sat dozing in the comfort of their hutch, a sound from the kitchen made them each sit up and listen.

It was a woman's voice – it was Betty!

The piggies were overjoyed. They leapt to their feet and wheeked loudly to her. The latch on the kitchen door lifted and in came Billy, with Betty close behind. She was beaming at the sight of them.

"Hello, my dears!"

She bent down close to see them through the wire mesh. She asked Billy to open up the catch at the side of the hutch, so she could give them each a stroke and a tickle around the ear, especially Hazel.

"We're taking them out into the garden, in a minute," Billy told her enthusiastically. "I've got it all set up."

Betty was shown out onto the lawn, where a table and chairs had been set up. A plump lemon and thyme cake, which she had baked and brought along that morning, had been placed on a plate in the middle of the table, along with a pot of tea.

She took a seat, and Mr Greenwood sat beside her. Betty smiled down at Madam Pom, who had crept out to sit at her feet. As always, her head was held high, in the expectation that the visitor would want to stroke her head. Of course, Betty obliged.

They sipped their tea in the sunshine, and watched as Billy came out, carrying the piggies in a wooden box.

He gently set it down upon the lawn, and lifted each guinea pig out, expertly sliding one hand under the front legs, the other under the back end. All four piggies were soon sitting upon the grass.

Hazel needed no encouragement. Immediately, she was off to explore. She was so excited to see the garden in daylight. What a different place it seemed from the moonlit world of the night before.

Alfie, Mama and Little Rufus soon followed close behind her, each equally keen to taste the fresh spring grass.

They all slowed down a little though, as they came across four large long yellow objects, which lay spaced out on the lawn in front of them. They were, in fact, the left-over ends of plastic gas pipes, which Billy had begged from some local workmen who were digging a road nearby.

Betty had mentioned to him how much guinea pigs enjoyed running through tunnels, so he had seized the opportunity when it presented itself.

Hazel was first, as always, to pluck up the courage to investigate. She poked her head into the relative darkness of one of the tunnels, and sniffed cautiously. All seemed fine, so she carried on inside the pipe, and kept on going.

Her small clawed feet could be heard tapping on the plastic as she scampered through to the other end. She emerged with a cheerful wheek of encouragement for the others to do the same.

They did so immediately, and each found they had a taste for it. Soon, all four piggies were scuttling through the tunnels, in one end, and straight out the other, only to repeat the exercise with the next plastic tube, just for the fun of it. They were having the time of their lives.

They were so joyous that they began to spring up in the air as they ran between tunnels, in a sort of cat leap, much to the amusement of the people watching.

"They're *popcorning!*" exclaimed Betty, in delight. "That's what guinea pigs do when they're extra happy!"

At this point, Molly had joined them at the table. Only (she pointed out to her father) because Betty made nice cake. Now, even she was laughing and enjoying the piggies' antics on the lawn.

Mr Greenwood smiled to himself. She was always so much calmer, and more civil, when Betty was around.

Eventually, the sky began to cloud over a little. Betty, John and Molly retired inside, whilst Billy gathered up the guinea pigs: an easy job to do as they had tired themselves out on the lawn. They were content to be scooped up and returned to their comfortable hutch, each piggy finding a place to spread out and relax in the sweet hay.

By nightfall, they were all sound asleep, all that is, except Hazel. She was feeling rather restless, and had slipped out under the loose wire mesh of the run, as before, and was now making her way out through the hole in the wall, into the moonlit garden.

Here she felt so different. Back in the hutch, it was hard to feel in any way 'special' with the boys teasing her.

Out here, in the silvery darkness, with the cool breeze in her whiskers, and the pale moon in the sky, it felt so different.

But when would being special mean something? When would the excitement begin? There was no one to ask. The next Full Moon was a whole month away, and the Queen would not return till then.

At that moment, her attention was drawn to something

shining in the dark sky. At first, she thought it was a blue star, but it was floating down towards her. It was a pale blue orb of light, which now hovered by her face.

"Hazel," said a soft voice.

The voice was familiar. Hazel realised it was Merriel, the mermaid.

"I'm here on behalf of Her Majesty," the soft voice continued. "She has a gift for you."

The guinea pig's heart fluttered, "For me?"

"Yes, for you alone. Be in the garden by sunrise – no later."

With that, the blue orb danced away into the night, leaving Hazel to wonder.

She gazed once more at the Moon, and wondered what it could be that the Moon Queen had in store for her. Perhaps the excitement was not so far away after all.

Chapter 10
The Small Orange Dog

A car-drive away from the village of Brierley Bramble, stood the town of Morecaston. If locals felt energetic, they could take the long walk there, through Lundy Woods.

In a neat little town house, on an estate in Morecaston, a young fluffy orange dog sat on the windowsill, looking out.

He was lonely.

He was very, very lonely and very, very bored.

It hadn't always been that way. As a tiny pup, he had had his brothers and sisters to play with, to chase and to snuggle up to. Life was fun. There was lots to do: running, jumping, tussling and battling over toys and socks.

But, one day, some strangers came into the house. The puppy was picked up, and driven away in a car.

A young couple had carried him into a strange house, with new smells and no familiar faces.

It was quite exciting, at first. He got lots of fuss and attention, and plenty of new toys. There was noise and distraction. He was taken out for a walk, returning home to a delicious bowl of food. He was happy.

Until that is, night came.

Then, it was a different story altogether. Once everyone had gone to bed, and the lights were out, the house became quiet and still.

Now, it was dark and lonely. Now, there were no other warm bodies to snuggle up to, no other ears to lick, no gentle reassuring sounds of his brothers and sisters softly breathing. Now, there was just a blanket, in a basket, in a deathly quiet house.

The little dog cried and whimpered. When no one came, he cried louder. Eventually, he howled at the top of his voice to make someone come.

They did, but there was no comforting stroke or a loving pat. He was scolded and told to be quiet. This happened night after night, until he learnt to stop.

In the day time, after the noise and bustle of breakfast, he was left in the house on his own, again.

There was absolutely nothing to do. So, he looked for something to stop the boredom. He climbed up onto the window sill to see the world outside, knocking off a vase, which shattered into pieces.

Next, he had a nibble of the leather settee, and it felt good. It helped relieve the pain of the teeth coming through his sore gums. It was also something to do, something to while away the long lonely hours, so he chewed it some more. A large piece came off in his mouth. He enjoyed playing with that, biting it into smaller pieces, and scattering them around the room.

When his owners came home, they shouted angrily at him. He had no idea why. He just cowered in the corner, with his ears flat.

Following that, he was shut out in the garden during the day. Still lonely, he barked at the postman to see if he would stop and talk to him. He barked at the children walking past on their way to school, in the hope that a small friendly hand might stroke him on the head through the fence. He heard dogs barking in the distance, so he barked back.

The weekends were great. His owners were there to keep him company, and he was happy. But, come Monday morning, once they were back at work, his loneliness returned. To relieve his stress, the little dog began to dig deep holes in the garden. The digging took his mind off things, and made him feel better. It used some of his pent up energy, and passed the time.

His owners were not impressed.

One day, out of desperation, he broke through the wooden fence, and squeezed into the neighbours' garden, where they kept a chicken coop. He had no idea, whatsoever, why the chickens made as much fuss as they did. He only wanted to talk to them, but they had to flap and squawk and cluck so loudly.

Yet more angry humans shouted. He was dragged home by the scruff and told off again. Once more, he was locked in the house.

The young couple had had enough. They now had a baby on the way and so a decision was made. An advertisement was placed in the newspaper.

He was offered free to a good home.

To the young couple's relief, a very pleasant, smartly dressed woman turned up at the door. She was all smiles, explaining how the dog was just what she was looking for – a welcome pet for her young son, Freddie. It was to be a surprise.

After he'd had his harness put on, the woman took his lead and, before walking him out to her car, assured the couple that of course she would take good care of him. Her son would *love* him. A nice forever-home was waiting.

The car ride took a while, but eventually, they came to a stop outside a house. The woman took the little dog out and greeted a rather scruffy looking man. Money changed hands, and the woman disappeared.

The man grabbed hold of the little dog's lead and shoved him into a cage in the back of a truck. The man clambered into the driver's seat. As the engine started, the little dog's ears lay flat. He did not like the strange smells inside the vehicle, and he did not like the man.

They drove for some time. When they eventually arrived at their destination, the little dog was on full alert. His senses warned him of something bad.

His nose told him they were near trees and fields. He could smell other humans, and many other dogs.

He heard barking. It was not the playful friendly barking of potential playmates, who wanted to say hello, but angry vicious barking, which made him fear for his life.

The back door of the truck was pulled open, the cage too, and the little dog's lead was seized. He was dragged out by the man. It was dark by now, but the little dog's keen eyes could pick out a large shed, from where the barking was loudest.

He had seen enough. He knew he had to get away.

The little dog's harness had always been loose fitting. He knew just how to angle his body, so it would slip off over his head, if pulled in a particular way.

This fact was about to save his life.

He trotted obediently next to the man, until the moment was right. Then, he pulled back abruptly, taking the man by surprise. With a swift wriggle, and a yank of his head, he was free.

The man yelled furiously, and tried to snatch hold of him, but the little dog was agile and quick. He took off like a small firework, scorching across the open fields nearby, away from the ghastly smells and sounds of the large shed. He ran and ran, until he could hardly breathe.

Exhausted, the little orange dog flopped down in an empty field, beneath a hedge. He closed his eyes, and fell asleep.

Chapter 11
The Gift

MORNING had not yet broken. As the rest of the house slept, Hazel crept down the ramp to the run beneath the hutch, and slipped out through the wire mesh.

With the dawn chorus in full swing, she found her way behind the cupboard, and popped through the hole in the wall, to emerge from behind the camellia bush into the fresh air of the garden.

The male birds were singing their hearts out, calling for love at the tops of their voices, and laying claim to their territories. Their full-throated warbles, whistles and trills surrounded Hazel and calmed her nerves.

The sun's golden sphere had yet to peek over the horizon and bring the day. A pale blue light filled the sky in anticipation of its arrival. Magnolia blossoms sweetened the air, filling it with a delicate scent, as Hazel breathed in deeply, momentarily closing her eyes, to enjoy the feeling of freedom she had craved for so long.

She waited expectantly. The Moon Queen's promised gift was still a mystery, waiting to be revealed.

Glancing over in the direction of the Moon Queen's statuette, at the far end of the garden, she half expected it to move and acknowledge her, but it stayed stonily silent and still.

Before long, the sky was brightened by a halo of orange, as the edge of the sun appeared behind the tips of the trees in the far distance. Hazel trembled slightly. The appointed time was here. Whatever was in store for her?

She froze. A rather large bird was sailing down from the sky. To a creature of her size, its wingspan looked huge. Hazel watched, full of trepidation, as it landed on the lawn, and began to walk slowly towards her. It was in fact a heron – a creature Hazel had never seen before in her life.

Her heart hammered in her chest as the large bird approached. She wanted to run back to the safety of the camellia bush, but stood firm, telling herself this must be from the Moon Queen.

"Good morning, Hazel," the heron said, most politely, as he drew close. "My name is Blake."

"G-good morning," she stammered in reply.

The heron turned his back to Hazel, folded his long legs beneath him, and lowered himself to the ground. He spread his wings out wide. "Hop on board," he said, to Hazel's astonishment.

Her stomach did a flip, but she swallowed hard, and gingerly approached the heron's wing. She tentatively put one trembling front paw onto its soft feathery surface. A reassuring warmth met her toes.

Barely able to breathe, Hazel stretched out another paw,

and clambered up, then across, onto his back. There, she fitted nicely into the space below his neck, where a thick twist of woodland vine awaited, to hold her in place. She slipped gratefully beneath it, and then settled down, between his beautiful grey and white wings, feeling full of anticipation.

"Hold on tight!" called the heron, over his shoulder, as he stood up.

Hazel clung on for dear life as Blake's wings began to beat the air, and the two of them rose up, up, and up, into the sky.

She shrieked with exhilaration as she saw the top of the silver birch tree appear below them. Together, they soared out of the garden of Bowood, with its orchard at the side, over the wildflower meadow, over the farm fields, past the old estate where the great hall had once stood, and over Lundy Woods.

Hazel's head was spinning with excitement. The highest she had ever been was the top level of the hutch, yet here she was now, sailing through the blue sky, far above the trees.

In time, her reeling senses settled down, and she began to enjoy the ride. The emerging sun cast a gentle warmth upon her back, and the spring air felt clean and pure as it slipped past her whiskers.

They were now out into open countryside. Below, the trees, fields, streams and hedgerows had been reduced to miniature size, whilst the houses had become tiny boxes. The greenery stretched out as far as the eye could see.

Hazel looked out over the earth below, and tried to take a picture to hold in her mind, forever. This was the big wide world she had always wanted to see. Never, ever did she imagine she would see it like this.

Before long, they were gliding over the nearby town. Most residents of Morecaston were still asleep, not yet ready to face the morning. The stillness of night had yet to be disrupted by the busy bustle of life. Windows and doors remained shut, cars sat on driveways, and few human beings were in sight.

The small guinea pig gazed in wonder at the scene below, whilst the heron tilted slowly, and began to curve through the sky.

Back on the ground, P.C. Jim Frankie, the Brierley Bramble police officer, was enjoying the early morning air as he cycled along a lane, flanked by green fields.

Sometimes he simply liked to escape into the solitude of nature before his day's duties began, to clear his head, and enjoy his thoughts.

He was a good man, but he did have one particular weakness. It was something which frequently earnt him a severe scolding from Mrs Frankie. He'd listen patiently as she warned him about calories, cholesterol and self-control, but he couldn't help himself.

He loved pies.

He adored the golden crumbly pastry which melted in the mouth to reveal the tasty filling inside. Nothing was more comforting and rewarding than sinking his teeth into a beautiful freshly baked pie.

Any such pastry delight could cheer his heart in an instant. It only took a sweet tangy apple pie, with the thrill of added blackberries, or a satisfying savoury vegetable pie, with extra thick gravy, to bring him close to tears of joy.

This fine spring day, he had a mouth-watering treat in store. When he had called in on Betty Albright, as he often did, just to check she was okay, she'd given him a wonderful apple pie. Its golden pastry was the most beautiful thing he had ever seen. The perfect pastry leaves on top were an exquisite extra touch. It was a piece of pure art.

This magnificent treasure had been wrapped in brown paper, and carefully placed, with great reverence, in the basket of his bicycle, just below his handlebars. The delicious aroma wafted up every now and again, making his stomach ache with anticipation. He pedalled happily along the empty country lane, whistling in the early morning sunshine.

As Hazel and the heron began their journey home, something caught the guinea pig's eye. Down below, in a field, sat something orange. It looked so out of place where it was, that she could not take her eyes from it.

"Blake!" she called to the heron, tugging on his feathers to gain his attention.

"Yes, Hazel?" he called back.

"Could we go a little lower? I need to look at something in the field below."

The heron dipped, and flew downwards, circling over the field, as requested.

At closer range, Hazel could see it was a little dog. She recognised the expression on its face all too well. It was the same haunted fearful expression she had worn herself, in the old hutch at Oakfield Lane. The dog looked frightened and alone.

Hazel desperately looked around for help, but there was no one in sight. Her heart sank – until her eyes fell upon P.C. Frankie, cycling along in the sunshine. He was separated from the field, where the dog sat, by a copse of trees.

Hazel recognised him at once. He had called in at Betty's house for a cup of tea, whilst the piggies were living in the kitchen. He had been a warm kind man who had spoken softly and stroked each of them gently on the head.

Right now, she was extremely glad to see him, but how was she to bring the dog to his attention?

As luck would have it, the police officer had stopped his bicycle, at the side of the road, in order to check on his pie. The brown paper wrapping had come a little loose at the sides, much to his concern.

Hazel glanced back at the little dog. He was now frantically digging a hole in the earth. She glanced around again, searching for inspiration.

And, then, it came to her.

A line of many starlings was sitting on the wire between some pylons, nearby. Hazel's brain whirred into action. "Blake, I need to speak to those birds over there!"

The heron was a solitary creature, who preferred his own

company, keeping well clear of other birds, but he recognised the urgency in her voice, and did as she asked. He tilted his wings, and flew over, close to the starlings.

"Hi there!" Hazel shouted to one of them. The starling stared back at her, startled, and ready to take flight.

"Are any of you hungry?" she called to him, as loudly as she could.

The starling's shock, at being spoken to by a guinea pig on a heron's back, was cancelled out by the question, as it seemed to concern food.

"Yes!" he shot back.

"Then look down there," Hazel called to him, gesturing to where the little orange dog was starting on another hole. "That dog is digging up lots of nice fresh worms and insects!"

The starlings reacted immediately. Wasting no time, they moved as one, swarming down to the field where the dog was disturbing the earth and stones.

The poor little creature was horrified to glance up and see a black cloud of birds descending upon him. He leapt up in a panic, and bolted for the safety of the trees.

Hazel held her breath, desperately hoping he'd run right through to the other side, towards the policeman.

She needn't have worried. The little dog had merely intended to take shelter amongst the trunks and branches, away from the starlings, until that is, his keen nose had picked up the tantalising scent of the apple pie, wafting on the breeze.

That caught the hungry animal's attention, and so did the sight of the police officer. The friendly little dog's ears perked up, and he raced forward, bounding out of the trees, towards P.C. Frankie.

As the policeman lovingly adjusted the brown paper around his pie, he nearly jumped out of his skin when a pair of paws landed on his leg. A small furry brown nose and a desperate pair of soft brown eyes looked up at him.

The little dog wagged his tail and licked the policeman's hand.

P.C. Frankie laughed and fondled his silky ears. He looked around, puzzled. "Where on earth have you come from?" he asked.

He had a horrible feeling that the dog had simply been abandoned. The police officer felt around in his pocket for the biscuit he knew was in there. The little dog wolfed it down, ravenously.

The officer sighed. The animal had no lead, no collar, and no identity tag. His cycle basket was full and there was nowhere to put him.

P.C. Frankie thought hard. Being an officer of the law, he was used to making hard decisions, but this was a tough one. Still, he knew what had to be done. He couldn't let emotions cloud his judgement.

"So sorry to leave you," he sighed, genuinely heartbroken.

As he cycled away, he felt pure misery. Not even the warmth of the spring sunshine could lift his mood, nor the tempting aroma of that beautiful pie. Each time he breathed in, he could smell it afresh.

So could the little orange fluffy dog, which now occupied the front basket, in place of the pie.

As P.C. Frankie cycled along, the little dog watched the world go by, panting happily and enjoying the fun of the ride.

Behind, at the side of the road, an equally happy family of crows was joyfully tucking into a beautiful golden freshly-baked apple pie.

Hazel cheered when she saw that her plan had worked, and the little dog was safe. The happy feeling continued, even though the thrill of the ride was coming to an end.

As they sailed back, over the open countryside, over the

fields, trees, streams and hedges, and then over Lundy Woods, Bowood appeared in the near distance. Already, it was feeling like home, and she was more than happy to see it again.

Blake swooped smoothly down into the garden, landing softly on the lawn. After thanking him warmly, and saying her goodbyes, Hazel shot a grateful glance in the direction of the Moon Queen's statuette.

She then made her way up the garden, heading for the camellia bush, so she could slip quietly back in, before breakfast was served.

Chapter 12
Skip

"WELL, he's perfectly healthy, I'm glad to say, "said Constance Clarke, the vet. "But he has no microchip, I'm afraid, so we have no way of knowing who his owners might be."

The little orange dog, sitting on the examination table, wagged his tail and licked the vet's hand. She smiled at him and stroked his ears.

P.C. Frankie scratched his head. Whatever was he going to do with the little fellow? He'd happily take him home, but his cat, Tabitha, would not take kindly to a new housemate.

There was the dogs' home, over in Morccaston, but the police officer could not bring himself to take the little dog there.

"We both know there's an obvious person here in Brierley Bramble who might help instead," said the vet.

P.C. Frankie smiled. Yes, indeed there was.

The Brierley Bramble police officer was on his bike once more, cycling in the sunshine in the direction of Bowood. As he travelled along, with the little orange dog in his front basket, Jim Frankie thought about John Greenwood.

In his mind's eye, he could still picture him very clearly as a young schoolboy. Smiling to himself, he thought back a number of years, to the incident involving John and the vicar's hat.

One day, the vicar in question (a visitor from the town of Morecaston) had made a special trip to Brierley Bramble Junior School, to lead a special Harvest Festival assembly.

The usual vicar of Brierley Bramble, a kindly old gent named Reverend James, was laid up in bed with a head cold. So, a substitute had been needed, much to everyone's disappointment, as the village vicar loved all people and animals alike, and was well loved in return.

This town vicar was quite the opposite. He was a most self-important man who enjoyed the sound of his own voice, and didn't like children very much at all. His session with the pupils seemed to them like it lasted forever, but he did finally finish by reminding them to pray every night, and to include their parents in their prayers.

A young John Greenwood had raised his hand and suggested that they should include their animals too – like the Reverend James would. The town vicar was not impressed. He had informed John, in a stern tone, that animals had no souls, and were only placed upon this earth to serve mankind. It was silly to even think of praying for them as if they were humans.

Young John had bitten his lip hard and seethed with anger. Being just a child, he was in no position to tell this reverend exactly what he thought of him.

When it was time for the town vicar to take his leave, he slipped on his coat, but could not find his hat. It was his absolute favourite, with the smart crimson feather in the headband, and now it seemed to be missing.

The children and the teachers searched high and low for the precious hat, but to no avail. It had completely vanished.

Only next day, did it strangely reappear. It was spotted, high up on a turret of the school roof, being worn at quite a jaunty angle by the metal rooster shaped weathervane, which had stood up there for years.

Everyone knew who the likely culprit was. There was only one child who was capable of getting up there. Yet, nobody said a word. No one had liked the vicar much anyway. Even the Reverend James had smiled when he heard the story.

On this lovely sunny day, the grown-up John Greenwood was at home, in his workshop, adding a coat of varnish to an ornate wooden table he'd finished that morning. His efforts were interrupted by a knock at the door.

He opened it up to find P.C. Frankie there, on his bike, with a small dog grinning up at him from the front basket.

Mr Greenwood didn't need to ask why he was calling. The dog, and the look on Jim Frankie's face, said it all.

"So, what's the story?" asked Mr Greenwood, as the police officer sipped his tea at the kitchen table, with the small orange dog sitting on his knee.

By now, Madam Pom had wandered in, and was staring in horror at the little dog.

P.C. Frankie explained the events of that morning, and looked at Mr Greenwood with pleading eyes. "I can't take the little fellow to the dogs' home, John – he's too small. He's so like the one you've already got. I thought he and Madam might make a nice pair."

Mr Greenwood shot a glance at Madam Pom and sighed with resignation.

Later that day, when Billy Greenwood arrived home from school, he was ecstatic to discover that they had acquired yet another new pet. "Really?" he exclaimed, barely able to contain his feelings. "He's *really* going to live with us?"

The fluffy little dog was soon joyfully jumping and playing with Billy in the garden of Bowood. Madam Pom came out of the dog flap, and settled down to watch them. She did not offer to join in, as she was far too dignified for such jumping around.

She merely lay down with her head between her paws, and grumbled to herself about having to share her home with yet another outsider. It was bad enough that she had to put up with those dreadful creatures in the outhouse, but now they were expecting her to live with another dog.

To make matters worse, this invader seemed to be a

Pomeranian too: he had the fluffy ruff around his neck, the long fur along his belly and the curled up fluffy tail.

One thing she was sure of, however, was that he was *no* pedigree. Madam Pom was a deep orange colour, with strands of black in her fur. *He* was a much lighter shade of orange, with much more white running through his coat. *And*, instead of a black nose and paw pads like hers, his were a *pale brown*. He could *not possibly* be registered with The Kennel Association of Great Britain!

Madam Pom was always very mindful of her pedigree status. Whenever she was out and about, she carried her head high, trotting along in a dainty fashion. 'Dignity at all times' was Madam's motto.

She had a tendency, however, to forget this whenever something distracted her sufficiently. Meal times always did the trick. Then she would wait anxiously for Billy to dish up her food, with both paws planted on his leg, yapping as loudly as her little voice would allow. As her dish was carried to the right spot on the kitchen floor, she would dance and twirl, and leap and spin on the spot in excitement, as she followed closely on Billy's heels.

She was so greedy that her food had to be served in a special 'slow-feeding' dish, full of circular compartments, to stop her wolfing it down in an instant. Afterwards, she would sleep off the food, snuffling and snorting as she slept.

As she sat now, watching Billy and the little orange dog cavorting on the lawn, she briefly pondered whether there might be a way to get rid of this latest creature. Immediately, however, she remembered her ordeal at the hands of the Moon Queen, and thought better of it. *This* one might be 'protected' too.

"Dad! Dad!" shouted Billy.

When Mr Greenwood stuck his head out of his workshop, his son exclaimed, "Dad, watch the way he moves!"

Billy threw a stick, and the little dog chased after it at top speed. Compared to Madam Pom, this dog had slightly longer, slimmer legs, and he seemed to skip sometimes as he ran.

"Let's call him *Skip*!"

"Sounds good to me," laughed his father, before returning to his work.

So now, the little orange dog had both a new home and a new name.

"Skip!" Billy called, as he and the little dog carried on their fun around the garden, "Come on, Skip!"

Madam Pom breathed in, and let out a deep sigh. Skip – what a ridiculous name.

Chapter 13

The Blackbird

IT was in the early morning, as daylight crept in, that Skip was awoken. He'd been snoozing peacefully in his special bed on the Bowood kitchen floor, his precious chew toy by his side, when he spotted something from the corner of his eye.

His whole body stiffened. Even in the dim light, there was no mistaking the familiar outline. It was his old enemy. It had come for him. He stared at it, with eyes full of hatred. He had known this day would happen. Well, it would not get the better of him this time.

This time Skip was ready, ready to deal with this tormentor once and for all. It was about to get its come-uppance. He would show it *no* mercy.

GGRRR! Skip was on his feet now. He was about to launch an attack. He gave the thing his most menacing sideways look. His growl was reaching a crescendo of anger. Then, he pounced, sinking his teeth into the furry offender.

It tried to resist, but Skip knew this was a fight he had to win. He clamped his jaws down harder. It struggled and struggled to evade justice...

Rudely awoken from her own peaceful slumber, Madam Pom watched with complete disdain, as Skip chased his own tail round and round in a circle. His jaws were locked upon the long fur at the end of his rump, and he spun around at increasing speed, growling ever more ferociously.

How ridiculous. She closed her eyes again, and resumed her sleep.

It had been two weeks since Skip had been adopted by the Greenwood family. Madam Pom's frosty reserve towards him had gradually thawed as the days had passed. She would never admit it, but the pompous pedigree was finding it surprisingly agreeable to have company of her own kind, even if he was only *half*-Pomeranian.

Of course, Skip was inferior and failed to meet her high standards. Even so, it was somewhat convenient to have another someone in the house who spoke her own special language. Walks were tolerable in his company, and having another furry body to sit alongside did feel fairly acceptable. It was not totally awful to have her ears and face licked on the odd occasion when she would allow it.

She might even admit it was faintly comforting to hear the sound of another dog breathing, in the dark kitchen at night, but then again – that would be preposterous.

Fortunately for him, Skip understood that Madam Pom was the boss. He had the good sense *never* to trespass onto her precious comfy bed. Consequently, she had reached the conclusion that she didn't particularly object to him living at Bowood. At least he was better than those creatures in the outhouse.

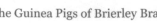

For his part, Skip could not be happier. The old life he had led, so full of loneliness, was now a distant memory. He had company, even in the darkness of night – the time he'd always dreaded the most.

Skip had been given his own soft plump bed, which had started out at a respectable distance from Madam Pom's. Little by little, he had dragged it a tiny bit closer each night, until it was just touching hers. He waited for her to notice and to growl angrily at him, but somehow, she never did. He would now drift off to sleep with the comforting sounds of Madam Pom snuffling, snorting and snoring close by.

Life at Bowood was wonderful for Skip. There was always company, and the garden was just the right size for a good romp around at full pelt, when he needed to let off steam.

Hazel could not believe her eyes when she saw the small orange dog, whom she'd helped from afar, suddenly appear in the outhouse. She was even more amazed when she learnt that he was living there permanently.

The piggies soon took to Skip. He was good natured and trusting. He was open and honest and full of the joys of life. He was also highly entertaining. They loved his boisterous side, and would laugh joyfully at him romping around the garden, at break-neck speed, chasing his own tail or barking wildly at Bruce the tomcat.

The Greenwoods had supervised him very carefully around the guinea pigs at first, watching his reactions closely, ready to intervene if necessary, but there was never any need. Like Madam, he showed no urge to harm them, and was now finally deemed trustworthy.

For Hazel, Alfie, Little Rufus and Mama, life was wonderful too. The outhouse was peaceful, cosy and warm, and there was plenty of human company. They especially loved their daily trips into the garden, under Billy's watchful eye at the end of the school day.

Of course, Billy wasn't to know about their other secret trips outside, when they'd slip out through the hidden hole in the wall, and access the freedom of the garden from behind the camellia bush.

It was now April, the greening month, and in the Bowood garden, the transformation of spring was well underway. The quiet, grey days of winter were now a distant memory. The sunlight was gaining warmth, and the daytime was beginning to hold its own with the darkness of night.

The new season had brought an eruption of colour to the garden. The grass was thicker and greener, and fragrant pink cherry blossoms bedecked tree branches. Dainty bluebells and forget-me-nots filled the flower beds, alongside tall crimson tulips and bright yellow poppies. The pretty purples of the bellflowers and the delicate columbines added to the paint box of colours. Birdsong filled the skies, and the world of nature seemed ever more alive.

After the arrival of the milder temperatures, a pair of blackbirds had nested in a small tree, near the end of the garden. The female bird was an attractive brown, but she was outshone by her mate, the handsome male, with his beautiful glossy black plumage and his bright orange beak.

They were frequently to be seen searching the garden for seeds and insects, turning over leaves and twigs, or listening carefully for worms in the soil. They each loved to take a dip in the birdbath, fluffing up their feathers and shaking off the refreshing droplets of water.

Now they were busy rearing their young. The mother bird had woven a fine nest from grass and hay. Their young could be heard each day noisily cheeping for food, their baby mouths wide open in anticipation. Both birds had been travelling endlessly back and forth to the nest with tasty morsels for their brood. The mother would eventually disappear to sit on the nest and keep them warm, leaving the father to carry on hunting for worms and insects.

One of their offspring was now old enough to have fluttered down from the nest, though not yet quite ready to fly. The fledgling was slightly fluffy, with an attractive reddish tinge on his speckled chest, making him appear a little like a robin. It would take some time before he took on the splendid beauty of his father.

At this present moment, he was hopping around the undergrowth, pecking at twigs, stones and soil, a little unsure of what to search for. Every now and again, his mother would help, by presenting him with a succulent worm or a juicy insect, which he instantly swallowed with relish.

Billy had spotted him early one morning after breakfast, as he filled up the birdbath and the hedgehog dish with fresh water. He kept Skip closely by his side, saying, "Leave," firmly to the small dog.

He needn't have worried; Skip watched the small bird with fascination, but showed no inclination to touch it. He'd rather play with it than eat it.

Billy knew to keep his distance from the bird. He also knew he couldn't interfere. This had happened before when he was much younger. On that occasion, his dad had explained to him, that Nature had to be left to do its job.

"That young blackbird will learn to fly in a few days," Mr Greenwood had said, "but until that time, he will be watched over by his parents, learning how to feed and how to survive on his own."

"Can't we put him back in his nest?" the younger Billy had asked his dad.

"No, Billy," Mr Greenwood had told him. "He would simply leave again. We'd do much more harm than good. Leave him to his parents. Just make sure the dog flap is locked for today, so Madam and Skip don't interfere."

Consequently, Billy wished the young blackbird good luck, and went off to get his school bag, taking Skip with him.

Mr Greenwood had a job to do on the other side of Morecaston that morning, and was in a rush, so Billy and his sister were ushered out of the door before he left – they both tended to dawdle on schooldays.

In all his haste, Billy had forgotten his intention to lock the dog flap. Once the family had gone, Skip was therefore able to slip back out into the garden, leaving Madam Pom sleeping off her breakfast and snoring heavily on her comfy bed.

Skip had already visited the piggies that morning to tell them what he'd seen, so now that the coast was clear, they too slipped out, using their hidden exit, and joined him on the grass. Together, they all began to amble along the lawn to see the young blackbird.

As Hazel, Alfie, Little Rufus and Mama neared the bottom, they spotted him, hopping and fluttering about beneath a leafy mahonia bush, still exploring the undergrowth of the garden.

At that moment, however, an alarm was raised. The mother blackbird, in a nearby treetop, had spotted Bruce the tomcat prowling his way along the top of the workshop roof, on the opposite side of the garden.

The mother made a loud constant repetitive call of increasing urgency as the cat slunk along. Hearing her cries, the flightless young bird had frozen still, beneath the bush. Soon the male bird appeared, and both parents twittered angrily at the sight of Bruce.

The tomcat himself had not yet spotted the small bird sitting hidden by the low hanging leaves. However, he recognised the distress calls of the parents, and knew they were likely to be protecting one of their young – he just needed to work out where it was. This could mean a nice tasty morning snack.

The piggies had frozen in alarm at the loud calls of the two blackbirds, but they had each seen Bruce, and knew exactly what would happen once he had detected the hiding place of the fledgling.

The parents would do their best to defend their offspring, but Bruce was a fearsome predator, and even the strongest blackbird stood little chance against him.

Hazel's heart thumped as she desperately scanned the garden for inspiration. Her eyes fell on something back near the house, and a plan began to form in her mind.

Meanwhile, Bruce was enjoying himself. He sat on the workshop roof, with his tail swinging lazily from side to side, and grinned down at the guinea pigs. *They* might be protected by the Moon Queen, but a juicy young baby bird would not – wherever it was. This could be fun, and he was feeling rather peckish.

Skip looked up at Bruce and barked angrily. Bruce merely looked back, unconcerned. The large wily old tomcat was more than a match for a small dog, like him. Bruce had sharp claws and could certainly defend himself in a tight corner.

As Skip continued his angry barking, Hazel whispered

urgent instructions to Alfie, Mama and Little Rufus. Once she had finished, they each turned around and began running up the garden, back towards the house, as quickly as their short piggy legs could carry them.

Bruce watched in amusement. The stupid creatures were clearly still afraid of him and were obviously running away in a panic. If only that wretched dog would stop making that infernal noise, he could concentrate on finding the young bird.

By now, Hazel and the others had got to where they needed to be – by the bright yellow plastic gas pipes which still sat on the lawn, near the house. The piggies loved running through these tunnels, on their visits outside, and now they might just save the life of one small bird, in danger.

One pipe lay in a useful position, parallel to the bottom of the garden. Under Hazel's direction, each piggy got behind it, and put the flat of their nose under its curved side, ready to push. Even Little Rufus got his small furry snout in the right position to do his bit.

"One, two, three – heave!" cried Hazel.

In unison, the piggies pushed and pushed with all their might, straining against the underside of the yellow pipe. It would not budge. The thick plastic was heavy, and was going nowhere easily.

"Skip!" shouted Hazel urgently.

The small dog stopped barking at Bruce, and raced up the garden towards them. He did as Hazel directed him, and got behind the pipe. They all tried again. This time, with Skip's efforts included, the pipe did move, but only just a little. Yet more help was needed.

Skip did some quick thinking of his own, and raced off towards the house, disappearing through the dog flap.

By this time, Bruce the tomcat was simply bemused. He may have been relishing the idea of a tasty morsel for breakfast, but like all cats, he was also highly curious, and was now eager to know what was going on.

He watched, spellbound by the sight of four guinea pigs trying to do something strange with a large yellow object.

Moments later, Skip came bursting back out from the dog flap, followed by an extremely angry Madam Pom. For a fleeting moment, Hazel did wonder what Skip could possibly have said to rouse her from her sleep and get her so fired up, but there was no time for that.

Madam Pom rushed to the pipe and angrily began to push at it with her forehead. Instantly, the others joined in, and soon the heavy plastic began to move.

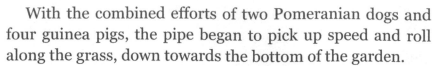

With the combined efforts of two Pomeranian dogs and four guinea pigs, the pipe began to pick up speed and roll along the grass, down towards the bottom of the garden.

Bruce watched, still baffled, as the pipe progressed, rolling, rolling, until it came to a halt, with one end facing the bush under which the young bird sat. Hazel judged they were now close enough for her plan to work.

Fortunately, fear stops an animal from moving, so Hazel and the others found the fledgling blackbird still sitting exactly where he was before, hidden by the leaves.

Now, came the next challenge. The pipe was close and would give the bird protection from Bruce, but how would they get him into it?

Hazel was given thinking time at this point, for Madam Pom had spotted Bruce on the fence, and was now barking angrily up at him. Skip went along to join forces with her, and provide backup.

Glancing at the yellow pipe, Hazel noticed bits of debris had stuck to its surface, from when it rolled along the lawn. There were strands of grass, tiny twigs, and most important of all, some small juicy worms. She dashed over, grabbed one of the worms in her mouth, and ran into the pipe, dropping it inside.

At the same time, Piggy Mama crept over to the fledgling to comfort him. The young bird was reassured by the soft tone of her motherly voice, and began to lose his petrified stillness. With her warm maternal body next to him, he relaxed and opened his mouth, instinctively hoping she might be about to offer him some food.

Now she had his trust, Mama knew she had to move quickly, for the parent blackbirds had begun their alarm calls once more. Despite the barking of Madam and Skip, Bruce had jumped down from the top of the workshop and was starting to approach. The whereabouts of the young bird had now become clear, and his stomach was beginning to rumble in anticipation.

Bruce was getting closer. Mama stretched up and nipped off a purple berry from the mahonia bush. The young bird instinctively opened his beak wide, enabling Mama to pop the berry in. She then began to run in the direction of the pipe, desperately hoping he'd follow. He did. He now associated her with food, and happily fluttered in her wake.

Mama entered the pipe as quickly as she could, jumping over the juicy worm, left by Hazel. The fledgling hopped straight in, and scooped up the worm – just as Bruce arrived on the scene.

Bruce looked closely at the pipe, and soon realised that he would be unable to fit more than his head inside. The fledgling was now sitting safely beyond his reach.

The tomcat hissed at the piggies in frustration, but stopped at that. He knew he could do nothing to them, protected as they were. Cursing, he withdrew and slunk back across the lawn, clambering back up onto the top of the workshop roof, his pride a little bruised.

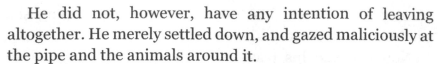

He did not, however, have any intention of leaving altogether. He merely settled down, and gazed maliciously at the pipe and the animals around it.

Hazel's heart sank. She guessed what he was up to. He was playing a waiting game. He knew full well that the young bird could not stay in the yellow plastic tunnel indefinitely.

Chapter 14

Bruce Enjoys Supper

ONLY ten minutes had passed in the Bowood garden, but already it felt like an eternity. Bruce was clearly going nowhere. He was quite comfortable resting on top of the workshop roof, basking in the morning sunshine, and dozing peacefully.

Skip and the piggies had settled down on the grass for a rest of their own, each with one watchful eye on the cat, and each hoping that someone would come up with an idea for what to do next.

Madam Pom however, had trotted off back up the garden towards the house, announcing that she was exhausted and needed a sleep.

As Hazel and Skip watched her go, Hazel asked, "Skip, whatever did you say to Madam, before, to get her to help us?"

Skip grinned. "I told her we were having a pipe pushing competition in the garden and Bruce was winning."

"Ah, that would indeed make her mad," giggled Hazel, admiring Skip's quick thinking.

"Yes, "replied Skip, "especially when I said Bruce had called her a baggy old fluff-head who couldn't even push a pipe down a hill."

Hazel giggled even more. No wonder the pedigree Pomeranian had rushed out through the dog flap in such a temper. She made a mental note to replay that scene in her head, the next time she needed cheering up.

With their youngster safe in the plastic tube, the adult blackbirds had now quietened down. Within a few moments, they had fluttered down to speak with the guinea pigs, and express their gratitude.

It was agreed that they would deliver food to the fledgling at regular intervals, and ensure he understood to stay well within his tunnel, until the cat was gone.

But, when would Bruce ever go? It would not do the young bird any good to stay cooped up all day, and he would never develop the ability to fly properly if he didn't practise using his wings.

Time passed. The sunshine disappeared behind the clouds, and cooler air began to chill the garden.

Hazel was beginning to shiver, partly from the cold, but mostly with a growing sense of anxiety. She crept over to Piggy Mama's side, as did Alfie and Little Rufus. When she looked around for Skip, Hazel noticed the thoughtful look upon his face.

To her surprise, he got up and walked over to the bottom of the workshop wall, where Bruce the cat was sitting.

"I have an offer to make," announced Skip, gazing up at Bruce. "Are you interested?"

"Well that depends," replied Bruce slowly, looking down

at the dog with an amused smile, "on how interesting the offer might be."

"How would you like a nice bowlful of tasty dog food for your supper tonight?" asked Skip. "It would be much more filling than one small bird."

Bruce's expression changed from amusement to one of intense interest.

Skip carried on, "If you agree to go now, and not come back till tonight, then you can have my dinner."

"*Your* dinner – how?" asked Bruce, a little suspiciously.

"I will help you sneak in tonight, when our humans are out of the way, and I promise you can help yourself," Skip told him.

A glint appeared in Bruce's eye. Now he was truly interested – for a cat to be *invited* into a dog's own home, to enjoy *his* supper, from *his* own bowl, right under the dog's own nose, would be the most splendid triumph of cat over dog! How deliciously humiliating would that be for a pooch?

Bruce smiled like a cat who'd enjoyed a whole month's worth of cream in one go. He stared at the earnest face of Skip, and grinned from ear to ear.

"Okay," he said, getting up onto his feet, "I will accept your offer."

In truth, he had become rather bored of sitting on the workshop roof, but he could not lose face by backing down in front of all these creatures in the garden. Now, he had an excellent reason for leaving, and an even better one for returning that night.

"I will go, as you ask, and I will be back at suppertime," he said smoothly. With that, he shot one final glance at the yellow plastic pipe, and disappeared from the garden.

Everyone breathed a huge sigh of relief as he went. Skip explained the deal to Hazel, Alfie, Mama and Little Rufus, who each looked at him sympathetically. They knew how much he enjoyed his food. Little Rufus, in particular, thought he had made a huge sacrifice, and did not envy him one little bit.

Now that it was safe, the blackbird parents encouraged the young bird to come out from the pipe, and to practise his flying. Before long, he was hopping around and exploring his surroundings once more.

The guinea pigs returned to the warmth of the house, slipping in through the wire netting of the run, back into the security of their hutch. All four were more than ready for a long sleep in the hay.

Sometime later, Billy arrived home from school, closely followed by Molly, and eventually, Mr Greenwood. Within a couple of hours, dinner was being served up for all. The piggies were brought a tasty selection of veggies; Skip and Madam Pom were given their bowls of meaty chunks with biscuit; and the Greenwoods sat down, at the big kitchen table, to discuss the day's events over a hearty stew and dumplings.

Once dinner was done, the Greenwoods left the table, and each withdrew to a different part of their home.

Having wolfed down her supper in the kitchen, Madam Pom now settled down on her soft comfy bed and immediately fell into a deep sleep, snorting and snuffling contentedly.

In the outhouse, Skip lay with his chin upon his paws,

looking wistfully at his bowl of lovely brown savoury chunks, sprinkled with delicious crunchy biscuits. His food was always served separately from Madam's so she couldn't tuck into his, as well as her own.

Skip's stomach rumbled loudly, as his ears lay miserably flat and his tail drooped in sadness. He felt famished, but he was a dog of his word, and would keep his bargain with Bruce, in order to protect the young blackbird.

With the family safely out of the way, Skip judged it was time to let Bruce in. He left the outhouse, crossed the kitchen, and stuck his head out of the dog flap.

As expected, Bruce was sitting on the patio, waiting for the small orange dog who was to give away his supper. At Skip's signal, he entered in through the dog flap, keeping a wary eye out for any humans, and followed Skip into the outhouse.

His eyes lit up as they fell upon the bowl, full of delicious food. He wasted no time, tucking into the soft brown chunks immediately, and savouring the delightful crunch of the biscuits between his teeth. Even a greedy cat like Bruce could not help noticing how fine the dog food was. This was high quality stuff – far superior to the supermarket rubbish his owners served up for him.

Once finished, he sat back and licked his lips with satisfaction. The guinea pigs had watched him feasting, from the upper level of their hutch, feeling so sorry for Skip.

He was a high-energy dog who needed his food, so his sacrifice was to be admired. His face was a picture of misery.

"Let me show you out," Skip said quietly to Bruce.

"No need, I know the way," replied the tomcat, who was only too happy to leave before humans appeared on the scene. He got up, and was about to go, but paused and looked at Skip.

"That was a mighty fine supper, dog. I shall be back at breakfast time for more – that way the baby bird will be safe for the whole day tomorrow."

He smirked, and then disappeared from the outhouse, silently crossing the kitchen, before taking his leave through the dog flap.

Chapter 15

An Empty Belly

THE guinea pigs looked at Skip, and their hearts went out to him. The sacrifice of his supper had not been enough. Now, Bruce would return in the morning, for his breakfast too.

Skip was sitting quietly, clearly miserable at the prospect of missing yet another meal. He got to his feet and walked slowly from the outhouse, into the kitchen, his ears flat and his tail hanging low. He lay despondent on his bed, next to his chew toy.

The piggies watched him go. "Whatever shall we do?" asked Hazel.

"Well, for a start, we can give him the chunks of carrot we saved from our supper," replied Mama. Even Little Rufus did not protest at this.

One by one, the piggies picked up the biggest chunk of carrot they could carry, before taking it down the hutch ramp, out under the wire netting, and onto the outhouse floor. They each dropped their chunk into Skip's empty bowl. It wasn't much but the carrot might just take the sharp edge off his hunger pains.

"We need to do more than this," remarked Alfie. "The little bird could take days to fly. Skip will starve at this rate."

The other piggies agreed. Hazel decided that now was the time to ask for help, from someone much more powerful than themselves. As the Full Moon was still days away, The Moon Queen could not be called upon yet – but surely, her sprites could.

The piggies waited for night to fall. Once it was dark and the Moon was visible in the sky, they slipped out from behind the camellia bush, and on to the patio.

Even though they knew they had the Moon Queen's full protection, within the boundaries of the garden, it was still an unnerving experience for the rest of Hazel's family to be out in the darkness of night. The piggies huddled together, and waited for Skip to join them, as he had said he would.

Once he appeared, they began the long walk down the

lawn, heading for the white marble statuettes, at the end of the garden. However, half way there, they were surprised to see four gently twinkling orbs of light appear before them.

A familiar voice spoke, "Do you need our help, Little Ones?"

Hazel immediately recognised the soft warm tones of Merriel, the water sprite.

"Yes please," she replied.

As the piggies and Skip looked on, one orb slowly transformed into the figure of Merriel, with her silvery blue mermaid's tail. Godfrig, Fion and Oro soon followed, materialising by her side.

"We've been watching you with interest," said Merriel gently. "You all did marvellous work in the garden today."

"You were there?" asked Hazel in astonishment.

"Then why didn't you help us?" blurted out Little Rufus, who had still not yet learnt to think before he spoke. He was instantly scolded by Mama, but Merriel merely laughed.

"I can understand you thinking that, Little Rufus, but you

were all managing simply fine on your own. We were proud of you."

"Besides," she continued, "We cannot meddle too much with the natural world. The Moon Queen will not permit it."

It was Godfrig who spoke next, a smile playing upon his cheerful bearded face, "We are here to help now. We recognise that the situation has become more serious."

"Yes, it has," agreed Hazel. "Is there anything you can do?"

"Yes," replied Godfrig, "Oro has devised a plan."

The slight boyish air sprite came forward and explained what they intended to do...

Once the plan had been explained, Fion, the fire sprite, placed numerous fire torches around the garden for extra light, whilst Godfrig dug up a good supply of worms and insects. Meanwhile, Oro found the blackbird parents roosting in the tree, and asked them to bring the fledgling to him.

Once found and brought into the light, the young bird was a little sleepy and confused at first. However, a good feed from Godfrig, and a little water dripped into his mouth from the clamshell of Merriel, changed all that. He was soon fully awake.

Oro was about to give the fledgling a flying lesson.

"Let's see what you can do," the air sprite said to the young bird. The fledgling fluttered his wings as hard as he could, and lifted a little from the ground. "Again!" urged Oro. The bird tried a second time, but with little further success.

"Okay," said Oro, we'll have another try, but this time I'll help.

The bird flapped his wings and tried to leave the ground. This time, Oro took a deep breath, and blew a large puff of air beneath the bird's wings. It made a huge difference. The light little body was lifted into the air, and carried along on the gust of wind created by Oro. He then landed softly on his feet, quite some distance from his starting point. Everybody cheered, and the young bird's face lit up.

"Fancy another try?" asked Oro.

Once more, the bird fluttered his wings, but with extra confidence this time. Once more, Oro blew air beneath his body to lift him up.

This was repeated a number of times. On each occasion, the fledgling rose higher, for longer, and travelled a greater distance along the garden. By now, the youngster was flapping his wings, rather than fluttering them, and was becoming stronger and more determined.

The next job was to teach him to fly high up into the air, well out of reach of any passing predator like Bruce, but by now the small bird was tired and ready to catch up on his sleep. It had been a successful lesson, but nothing more could be achieved that night.

It was agreed that he would receive further lessons the following evening. At this moment, he needed rest, so his mother led him back to the safety of his night time hiding place.

As Little Rufus was yawning too, Mama took him back to the house, leaving Hazel, Alfie and Skip to say goodbye to the sprites.

"Thank you," said Hazel. "We're so grateful for your help."

"You're very welcome," replied Merriel. "We're always here for you if you truly need us. Just use us sparingly, and we'll help when we can. We will see you tomorrow, after dark."

With that, the sprites disappeared, and the fire torches went out, leaving the garden quiet and still once more.

By the light of the Moon, Hazel, Alfie and Skip ambled back up the lawn towards the house. Skip headed for the dog flap, whilst the two piggies slipped through the hole behind the camellia bush.

Chapter 16

The Betrayal

As the next day dawned, the sky was overcast, and a fine drizzle of rain had set in. The leaves in the garden began to droop under the weight of moisture, and water dripped a little sadly from the ends of their tips.

The weather suited Skip's mood, for he knew he didn't even have breakfast to look forward to. Bruce would be arriving, once the humans were out the way, expecting a repeat of the previous day's feast. Skip would have no choice but to sit back whilst the cat greedily wolfed down the contents of his bowl.

The guinea pigs had made an agreement to save all their veggies for Skip. They breakfasted on sweet hay and dried food, but left the carrot, cucumber and apple pieces for him. He was grateful, of course, but his belly longed for his savoury chunks and biscuits.

Eventually came the sound of the front door slamming shut, indicating that the last member of the family had left Bowood. Skip opened the dog flap, to see Bruce sitting there – this time, with company.

To ensure Skip's total humiliation, Bruce had brought along another cat to share the fare on offer. It was rather a scruffy scrawny ginger cat. Skip did not like the look of him at all.

However, with no other choice, the dog reluctantly let them both into the kitchen. He was about to lead them past the bed where Madam Pom snored heavily, when Bruce announced, "It's all right, we know the way!" Smirking, he and the other cat dashed off into the outhouse, and set about demolishing Skip's breakfast.

The guinea pigs were horrified to see two separate cats devouring poor Skip's food, and sought refuge in the safety of their upstairs nesting box.

In no time at all, Skip's bowl was empty, but instead of taking their leave through the kitchen, Bruce and his companion merely stretched out upon the nice warm floor, as if they were going to settle down for a sleep. Skip stared at them in disbelief.

"It's rather wet and cold outside," Bruce announced. "It would be rather agreeable to take a nap right here in the dry, don't you think, Ginger?"

The other cat smirked at him and nodded, "Oh, yes."

"And I was thinking," continued Bruce, "how much nicer it would be, if we were to eat our food from Madam Pom's bowl tonight."

That was the final straw. Skip leapt to his feet in outrage, and began barking ferociously at the two feline intruders. The angry tone of his barks alerted Madam Pom, who awoke with a start, and leapt to her feet. She rushed through to the outhouse, barking as loudly as her voice allowed.

She couldn't believe her eyes when two cats came streaking past her, through her kitchen, out through her dog flap, and off into her garden. The outraged Pomeranian raced out through the same flap to ensure they were off the premises.

Upon her return, an explanation was demanded, and Skip had to give it. The guinea pigs came out of hiding to provide moral support, as the poor little dog tried to explain.

Madam Pom was speechless as she listened to what had been going on. Bruce had been *inside* her house! She was beyond angry, and barked furiously at Skip, before flouncing off in a terrible sulk.

Hazel and the other piggies sat by Skip's side to commiserate with him. One thing was clear – the situation could not go on. Bruce was simply going to demand more and more.

At that moment, they were interrupted by the familiar loud distress calls of the blackbirds in the garden. The piggies rushed to their hole in the wall, and Skip dashed to the kitchen dog flap.

All five animals emerged to see the scrawny ginger cat in the middle of the lawn. It had returned to the garden, alone. The cat was low to the ground, in a hunting position, and was stalking the young blackbird, which stood on the grass, petrified.

The fledgling had frozen at the sound of his parents'

urgent calls. He could see the ginger cat approaching, but was now too terrified to move. The cat was getting closer and closer.

Skip and the guinea pigs charged down the garden, as fast as they could, but the ginger cat had already begun its final run towards the small bird.

As it was about to pounce, a streak of black feathers shot across the garden and swooped in front of the cat's face. A blur of angry black wings and an orange beak pecked at its head, and halted it in its tracks.

It was the fledgling's father.

Infuriated, the ginger cat swatted at the blackbird with its front paw and sent him flying to the ground. Now the ginger cat had a choice – did he want to eat the youngster, or its father lying winded on the lawn? He was about to go for the bigger option, when a hissing sound interrupted him from behind.

It was Bruce. The tomcat had reappeared in the garden, and was incensed to discover that he had been double-crossed by his companion. A terrible feline battle then ensued, with clumps of dark grey and ginger fur flying around in the air. The ginger cat was coming off by far the worst, and soon extricated himself from the situation to make a run for the workshop roof. He scaled it, in an instant, and bolted off into the distance, closely followed by an enraged Bruce the tomcat.

Hazel, Skip and the other three piggies had been too shocked to react to what they saw. They could merely stare at the spectacle in horror.

Despite her fear, however, the mother blackbird had flown down to her young one, and had begun ushering him to a place of safety.

Her arrival seemed to wake the fledgling from his frozen stupor of fear. He flapped his wings as hard as he could, and to her total surprise, rose up into the air, higher and higher and higher.

He then flew over to a tree, and sat on its branch, letting out a loud tweet, feeling rather proud of himself.

The piggies watched him go, and wheeked in delight. His father, now recovered, gazed proudly up at him, whilst Skip barked in excitement. His mother happily flew up to sit beside him on the branch.

It would seem that Oro's flying lessons had paid off.

Later that day, when the family was home, and food was dished up for all, Skip tucked into his food with extra relish, savouring every wonderful mouthful. The chunks tasted divine, and the biscuits had the most heavenly crunch imaginable.

Afterwards, he settled down on his comfy bed for a long luxurious sleep, content to listen to the sound of Madam Pom's deep, thunderous snoring.

Chapter 17

Her Majesty Returns

A few days later, the Full Moon returned, and so did the Moon Queen. When night had fallen, the four guinea pigs and the two Pomeranian dogs were assembled in the garden, before her.

By the flames of Fion's lantern, with her four sprites around her, the Moon Queen listened as each in turn spoke. First, Skip was introduced to her as a new member of the household. Then, with Hazel taking the lead, the animals each recounted their role in the rescue of the young blackbird. The monarch listened patiently, though Hazel rather suspected that Her Majesty already knew the whole story.

The Moon Queen's face, as always, remained calm and serene, but the moonstone atop of her staff gleamed brightly, indicating her pleasure at the good work they had done.

Eventually, Little Rufus began to yawn, and the Moon Queen decided it was time for them all to retire, except that is for Hazel, with whom she wished to speak further. Mama led the way, as Skip, Madam Pom, Alfie and Little Rufus returned back to the house, leaving Hazel behind.

"You have come such a long way, in such a short space of time, Hazel," said the Moon Queen. "I am proud of you, and

I am glad you are already making the most of your new start in life. What you did for the young blackbird was both kind and brave."

Hazel's heart swelled with pride at Her Majesty's words.

Against the dark night sky, the Moon Queen had a silvery aura, like a shining halo of light encompassing her entire figure. The piercing gaze of her silver blue eyes, beneath her pale lids, suggested to Hazel that they saw everything, and nothing could be hidden. The monarch looked deep into Hazel's small eyes, as if reading her thoughts.

"Life is so much better for you now, Hazel. You and your family are safe and warm, and never need fear hunger again – yet I feel there is a sadness within you," she said gently.

Hazel looked down. "I'm happier than I have ever been, Your Majesty." She swallowed, feeling guilty after all the Moon Queen had done for her and her family. "It's just that..." Again, she hesitated. "Your kind words mean so much to me, but I wish Piggy Papa was here to be proud of me too. I just miss him so much. I miss hearing his voice. I miss sitting at his side. I miss the smell of his warm fur."

Emotion was getting the better of her. She could not bring herself to say the one thing she needed to. It seemed so wrong to even think it, never mind express it, but the truth was she felt angry with Papa – incredibly so. Why did he have to leave them?

Despite her best efforts to control it, a deep sob shook Hazel's entire body and stopped her from continuing. It was as if a cork had been removed from a bottle. All her held-back emotions came pouring out, and she could no longer hold onto them.

As she wept, the sprites crept around to comfort her. Fion stroked her ears, Godfrig dried her tears with his shirt sleeve, Oro fanned her a little with his wings, and Merriel dabbed cooling water on her forehead.

Once calm, Hazel kept her gaze low, not daring to look at Her Majesty, for fear she would be angry with her. To her surprise, the Moon Queen spoke very tenderly. "Hazel, your anger is natural, but I can assure you your father has never truly left you, and *is* very proud of you."

Hazel blinked up at her, puzzled. The Moon Queen continued, "The loved ones we lose are never gone. They are always there, right beside us. I promise you – your father sees everything that you do."

Hazel sat motionless, unsure of what to say.

"Fion," said the Moon Queen, "pass me your lantern."

After the fire sprite had done as instructed, the Moon Queen held the light aloft, saying to Hazel, "You see this flame? Imagine this is the spirit of your father. Each time you recollect happy memories of him, and think well of the time you once shared, his flame will burn brighter, and you will feel more aware of his presence." She smiled and passed the lantern back to Fion.

"You will see him again one day, Hazel. Till then, keep his spirit strong with your thoughts."

The guinea pig felt as if a weight had been lifted from her shoulders. So often she had tried not to think about Papa as it hurt so much; he just seemed absent from her life forever. Now, the Moon Queen had changed all that.

She suddenly felt exhausted. The Moon Queen recognised her weariness, and bid Hazel to retire to bed, adding, "I am here for the duration of the Full Moon. If you need to speak with me further, you know how to find me. Merriel and Fion will accompany you back to the house."

The two sprites walked Hazel back up the garden, taking their leave of her at the camellia bush.

As she slipped back under the wire mesh of the run and crept up the ramp into the hutch, Hazel felt sure she could sense the presence of Piggy Papa right beside her.

Chapter 18

The Journey

BRIERLEY Bramble had welcomed in the new month with traditional May Day celebrations.

A young May Queen had been led through the village, in a white dress, a fresh flower garland in her hair, and children had woven their way around a maypole on the village green, colourful ribbons in hand.

A couple of weeks on, Brierley Bramble was now lush with green. Gentle bird song was a constant backdrop to everyday life, and the sun shone with an increasingly generous warmth.

Madam Pom had been insufferable all week. She'd been walking around with her nose in the air and her head held high, behaving in an even more pompous, self-important manner than usual. The smug look on her face suggested she was harbouring a delicious secret which no one else shared. She made frequent comments about being 'too good' for Bowood, and constantly criticised Skip and the piggies for being 'vulgar' and 'unsophisticated'. The guinea pigs kept out of her way as much as possible. Even good natured Skip steered well clear.

That morning, she had disappeared into the garden, and everyone had heaved an enormous sigh of relief. Without her, the house was calm and peaceful. In fact, it was unusually so for a Saturday. There was no flouncing and shouting from Molly, no sounds of Mr Greenwood sawing or hammering, and no sounds of Billy laughing and playing with Skip. The Greenwoods had gone to a family wedding in another part of the country, and would not be back until later the next day.

Hazel had listened in on recent conversations, and knew that Betty would be arriving later, to feed them and look after them overnight. No one was concerned therefore, by the quietness of the house or the absence of human life. Instead, the piggies were enjoying a good lie in, Skip too. Hazel snuggled down in the fresh hay, supplied by Billy that morning, and snoozed a little more.

Out in the garden however, a certain pedigree Pomeranian was up to no good. She was putting final preparations into place. At last, the day that she had been waiting for had arrived.

Madam Pom had a plan.

Bowood, she had decided, was simply not big enough for a dog of her supreme pedigree breeding. Its walls could hold her back no longer. Her destiny was to be out there in the big wide world, which she had so often dreamed of.

Recently, she had discovered a large gap in the bottom of the hedge, on the orchard side of the garden. She had happened upon it whilst following the scent trail of a hedgehog in the undergrowth. Tall clumps of grass had hidden this from view, so she alone knew of its existence. This gap was wide enough for her to squeeze her whole body through.

Once she heard about the Greenwood's trip away, she knew the time had come to act. With just a little effort, she was able to push her way through the hedge and out into the orchard. From there, the five bar wooden gate, which led to the wildflower meadow, was easy to slip through – so she did just that.

Ha, ha, she'd done it! She'd broken out! She was *Madam Pom Pom de Belvedere Dancing Queen,* highest ranking Pomeranian of the National Kennel Association, now Queen of the Open Road. Freedom was hers!

She trotted along with a gleam in her eye, and a twinkle in her toes. She held her head high. Her ears were pert, and her fluffy curly tail stood tall and proud. She was monarch of all she surveyed. The air was *so* sweet to her senses. The breeze felt *so* fresh in her fur. Oh, how pleasantly the birds were singing, how blue the sky appeared, how green the trees!

It was the town for her, where all the glamour was, the sophistication, and the culture. Each time she had seen Morecaston, from the window of Mr Greenwood's truck, she'd always felt so drawn to the colour, the excitement and the crowds of people.

Once she was out there, once she was no longer cooped up in a dull little village, she'd be seen by so many more people – people who would appreciate her magnificent qualities. Who knew what the future might bring? She could feature on the front of magazines, or star in television commercials. She was *bound* to be snapped up as a model, for she *was* a pedigree Pomeranian, with a beautiful bushy tail and a most luxurious fluffy ruff. She just needed to be noticed by the right people.

Madam picked up her pace.

She was soon through the wildflower meadow, heading into a field of wheat. Madam Pom threaded her way between the cow parsley, velvet grasses and wildflowers which bordered the young green stalks of wheat.

This field, and those beyond, belonged to Farmer Jack Lewis. In contrast to the modern commercial farming around Morecaston, he continued with the traditional methods of agriculture. No harsh pesticides or herbicides touched his land. The strips of wildflowers, enjoying life along the borders of his wheat fields, bore testament to that.

He allowed cornflowers, poppies and other 'weeds' to grow amongst his crops. Unlike the sterile, chemical-drenched wheat fields, found on the town side of Lundy Woods, Farmer Lewis's fields teemed with wildlife: from hares, partridges and rabbits, to voles, field mice, red kites and buzzards.

By now, Madam Pom was panting rather heavily. Her noisy breathing caused any resident creatures to keep their distance, so she passed through with no hinderance of any kind. Each time she felt tired, she thought of the bright lights and fame which awaited her, and struggled on. As she padded out of the wheat field, she trotted over the pastures, giving the grazing cows and sheep a careful wide berth, and made her way to Lundy Woods, lying just a short way ahead.

One last effort was required to cover the distance uphill, where a path led into the woods, guarded by a rather sharp prickly blackthorn tree...

Chapter 19
Morecaston

BETTY was on a trip to Morecaston. She was meeting her friend, Jean, for lunch at the fancy tea rooms, followed by a stroll around the shops. This was to be the first time without her walking stick, her ankle being so much stronger now.

She was thoroughly looking forward to her day. A bus ride to the town was always a mini adventure. In the late spring sunshine, the view from the bus window was captivating for Betty. She never tired of seeing it. The open countryside extended as far as the eye could see, ending at the green of Lundy Woods. Eventually, the road curved around the woods, passing within a field's distance of its outer trees. It was then a straight road through to Morecaston, passing a few more fields of green.

Betty watched the world go by and smiled in delight.

It was an especially busy shopping day in Morecaston. Spring sale signs advertised massive savings in all the shop windows, and people were making the most of it.

Madam Pom was becoming increasingly weary as she continued her epic journey. However, she was determined not to fade now – it was essential to keep on going. She struggled through the wheat fields on the edge of the town, as quickly as she could – the lack of wildlife made them eerily quiet. Once out, she followed her keen sense of smell, and soon found a road leading to the main high street. She knew this was it, her chance to be spotted, to be discovered. No longer would she be hidden from sight in Brierley Bramble.

She breathed in deeply, held her head up high, and trotted out into the throng of people.

The going was tough at first. She had to thread her way past scores of feet, narrowly avoiding being stood upon, on numerous occasions. Before long, she found a space on a wooden box outside a shop, and hopped on.

"Aw, what a pretty dog!" said a little girl within moments. A small hand stroked her head, but the child was soon ushered away by her busy mother. Madam Pom proudly soaked up the compliments she received from the various passers-by. An hour later, however, she was becoming rather overheated in the sunshine, and extremely thirsty.

Madam Pom jumped down from the box and set off in search of water. The thick forest of legs was still hard to navigate her way through. Shoes, boots and trainers caught her delicate paws or threw her to one side. At this level, people just didn't seem to notice her. They were either too busy talking or had their eyes glued to their phones. No one had time to look down.

The Pomeranian's regal poise was beginning to slip away. How noisy and fierce the traffic was. How busy the pavements were. How scary the world had become.

Business was not going well at *Morecaston's Premier Photographer's Studio*. Despite prices being slashed on 'family fun photos', none of the busy crowd had stepped through the door. The owner, Doreen, sighed heavily. The digital age was seriously damaging her business, and the advent of the 'selfie stick' had just about finished it off altogether. The offer, of a family portrait with a drastic fifty per cent discount, displayed in the window, had persuaded no one to enter the shop.

She stood in the doorway of her studio, bottle of water in hand, breathing in the fresh air, and thinking over her problems.

Doreen's gloomy thoughts were interrupted by a sound at

her feet. What was this? A small fluffy dog was looking up at her, or rather, at her bottle. It licked its lips and looked hopeful.

Doreen smiled and bent down, pouring water into her hand and offering it to the dog. Madam Pom bent forward, intending to sip delicately from the water, as a dignified Pomeranian should, but she was so overcome by her raging thirst, that she gulped it down voraciously in seconds.

"Aren't you a pretty little thing?" Doreen said. She stood up and glanced around the street, expecting to see someone looking for their dog, but no one was. It had no collar, was clearly hungry and thirsty, so must be a stray.

As Doreen stood up, the dog strolled past her into the shop as if she had a natural right to do so. She had such an air of dignified expectation, that she reminded Doreen of an aristocratic lady she'd seen in a film the day before. "Do come on in, *Duchess!*" she laughed.

Madam Pom had been so desperate to cool down and escape the crowds, that she wasn't going to wait to be invited. She now lay down upon the cool floor and panted. Doreen filled a dish with the rest of the cold water and watched the dog drink. An interesting thought crossed her mind...

"Hmm, if I help you, Duchess, then I think you might just be able to do me a favour in return. Hang on there, a moment."

Doreen slipped out of the shop door, pulling it to behind her. Ten minutes later she was back, with a tin of dog food in one hand and a bag of items in the other.

Madam Pom ate heartily from the saucer placed in front of her. It was not her usual quality food, but she was quite frankly starving and would have eaten just about anything.

With a full belly, she lay down to sleep, snoring contentedly. Eventually, she was gently awoken by Doreen, partly because her snoring was steadily increasing in volume, but also because the photographer's preparations were now in place.

Madam sat up as a nice soft brush was put through her fur. What a lovely sensation. At last, someone was giving her the respect she deserved. This lady clearly recognised her true worth.

With the encouragement of a small dog biscuit, Madam was led onto a large beautiful silky cushion, where a bright light shone down upon her. Madam Pom's heart began to race. This was it! She knew the black object pointing at her was a camera. She was about to have her photograph taken – by a proper professional!

The brush once again fluffed up her fur. A small golden object appeared in Doreen's hand. As soon as Madam saw it, she felt beside herself with excitement. She let out a whimper of sheer joy. For, in Doreen's hand, was a tiara. It was only a plastic one, from the toy shop over the road, but to Madam, it was a crown of pure gold, inlaid with the most precious jewels.

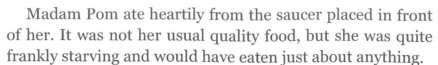

As it was held over her head, the world moved in slow motion for Madam Pom. In her mind, angels began to sing, and a heavenly light shone down upon her, as if she was being blessed by the divine. It was her coronation. The crowning moment of her life...

"Now, hold still, Duchess," said Doreen gently, as she pressed the button on the camera.

The sound of the high-speed shutter closing, again and again, was music to Madam's ears. She had heard it on the television when celebrities were surrounded by paparazzi cameras flashing and clicking.

She held her head high and proud, breathing deeply, living in the moment, her heart swelling with pride and emotion.

"Good girl!" announced Doreen, finally putting the camera down. "I think that will do for now."

The tiara was lifted from Madam's head, and placed on a nearby surface, where she continued to gaze in wonder at it.

"You deserve a rest now, Duchess," smiled Doreen, running her hand over Madam's head. She carried the camera over to her laptop, and plugged it in. Madam Pom settled down on the silk cushion and closed her eyes. Drained of all emotion, the aristocratic dog sank into another deep sleep, snoring loudly.

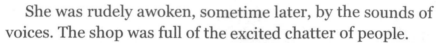

She was rudely awoken, sometime later, by the sounds of voices. The shop was full of the excited chatter of people.

A large picture of Madam now adorned the window of the shop, along with the headline: *Come and have your picture taken with our beautiful Duchess!*

An ornate couch had been pulled into the centre of the shop, with the camera trained upon it. A backdrop had been placed behind the couch, showing the inside of an expensively decorated room, worthy of a palace. Madam Pom soon found herself seated on the couch with a little girl, in a princess dress. They both wore tiaras, with pink feather boas wound around their necks. The camera whirred into action.

Next came a family of four, followed by a family of three. Two young men were next onto the couch. They posed, all piercings, tattoos and smiles, with Duchess in pride of place between them.

Madam Pom was ecstatic. She had found the public adoration she always knew was rightfully hers. She was the centre of attention. Her Pomeranian grin was wide and cheerful.

Doreen was feeling equally blessed. Her card payment machine had been in use non-stop, and it was still only early afternoon. Already the day had been a resounding success. There had been no time to eat or drink, her feet were aching, her back was sore, yet she was over the moon.

Still, there was no rest to be had just yet. The May crowds

were still filling the streets outside her door, and more business could still be had.

She was right. As the lunch time pubs emptied, more customers piled in. Although, their tastes were rather different. The first customer wanted Madam's beautiful tiara swapped for a red bow tie. The next one wanted her in a pair of star-shaped sunglasses. After that, she had to sit inside a huge handbag with a flower behind her ear.

Madam Pom was beginning to feel rather grumpy. The glare of the lights was feeling much less divine, and she was tiring of the many pairs of hands ruffling up her lovely fur. Sitting on so many laps was becoming hot and exhausting.

The final straw was not the unicorn horn, strapped to her head with the sprinkling of glitter, nor the black cape requested by the giggling pair of Goths, but was, in fact, the false rubber smile which she was expected to hold in her mouth, whilst sitting across the laps of a loud middle-aged couple. Their beery breath and childish giggles were just too much to bear. Her Pomeranian grin was long gone.

As they paid for their picture, she jumped to her feet, slipped out the open door, and ran down the street, heading back out of town.

Madam Pom kept on running until she reached the sanctuary of Lundy Woods. Once in, her whole demeanour changed in an instant. Her body relaxed, her breathing slowed down, and her pulse stopped racing. Her senses were no longer being assaulted by the car fumes, the deafening noise of the traffic, and the general unrelenting hubbub of people.

The solitude of the woods was bliss, and the lyrical birdsong a soothing balm for her shredded nerves. Her paw pads, sore from trekking the hot hard pavements and tarmacked roads, were now grateful for the cool woodland floor, cushioned with fallen leaves and vegetation.

Even the light was gentler on her eyes. The canopy of the trees had yet to take on their close dense summer fullness. Sunlight gently filtered through the young leaves of varying shape and texture, creating patterns of light and shade.

Exhausted, Madam Pom sank down, shut her eyes, and began to snore.

Chapter 20

Into the Woods

MADAM Pom's arrival had been noticed. The trees were listening.

The trees, Nature's background to life on Earth, stood calm and steady, slowly living life at their own pace, whilst human beings hurried and scurried about, busy in their modern world. Beneath their branches, generations of Man had lived, loved, played, fought and hunted. Through the ages, the trees had watched and listened, recorders of time, keepers of secrets.

The trees were talking.

Deep beneath the soil, where the tree roots reached down into the earth, the underground network was communicating. Delicate tendrils of fungi, interlaced between the roots, were Nature's transmitters, passing a measured steady stream of information, noting an intruder's presence, assessing the threat, signalling to others.

Many signals of alarm were now being sent. The snoring of Madam Pom was causing quite a stir. The animals of the wood stopped whatever business they were about, each one startled by the thunderous sound reverberating around the trees. The birdsong was shocked to a halt, rabbits scuttled back to their warrens, magpies called out warning rattles, and squirrels crashed through the leafy branches, higher up into the safety of the treetops.

None of this, however, disturbed the deep, exhausted slumber of Madam Pom.

Near the edge of the woods, the bus carrying Betty back from her daytrip to Morecaston was making its way to Brierley Bramble.

As the bus sped along the road, a strange noise came from

its engine. The noise became louder and louder until the vehicle came to a juddering halt by the kerb.

The driver sighed in exasperation, and radioed the depot. He soon announced that an alternative bus would be despatched as soon as possible. In time, a tow truck arrived to remove the bus, leaving Betty and the rest of the passengers to await its replacement at the roadside.

The few stranded passengers waited as patiently as they could, chatting, reading newspapers or browsing their phones.

As Betty waited, a boy of junior school age approached her, tugging on her sleeve and looking up into her face with big earnest eyes, slightly brimming with tears.

"Excuse me," he said in a trembling voice, "could you help me, please?"

"Of course," replied Betty, looking down at him with concern.

"It's my little sister, Lucy," he explained. "I promised Mum I'd get her home safely, but she's just run off into the woods."

"Oh dear!" exclaimed Betty.

The boy's chin quivered as he carried on, "Mum always says it's best to ask a lady for help when I'm in any trouble."

Betty glanced over at the queue of people waiting for the bus. There was a mother trying to cope with an agitated child; a couple of young boys with their hoods up, engrossed in their phones; and a few elderly folks, who looked as tired as she felt. No point in asking for any help there.

Betty knew Lundy Woods like the back of her hand. She had foraged there for plants and flowers since she was a young girl, so they held no fear for her, but they certainly might for a child, lost and alone. Despite her tired legs, Betty picked up her shopping bag.

"You come with me and we'll look for her. What's your name?"

"Jack," came the tearful reply.

Together, Betty and Jack crossed the field leading to the edge of the wood. As they entered between the trees, Betty cast her eyes around for any sign of life. Everywhere was fairly quiet, apart from birdsong. "Hello?" she called out.

They scanned the area, with Betty calling over and over again. There seemed to be no sign at all of the little girl.

The further they went into the woods, the more the boy hung back. In his hand was his mobile phone. Unseen by Betty, his eyes were watching his screen, taking no notice of his surroundings, as if he was expecting a communication. Finally, his phone buzzed.

The boy's expression now changed. A sly grin crossed his face. "Look over there!" he shouted to Betty. As she did so, he charged up behind her and pushed her with all his might. She toppled forward, painfully catching her weak ankle, and landing on top of her shopping bag in the undergrowth.

"Sorry, Missus, got to go!" shouted the boy over his shoulder, as he raced away, back out of the woods. It took his young legs just minutes to cross the field and reach the road, where the replacement bus was just pulling up to the kerb.

He was greeted with high-fives by his two friends, Ronnie and Reggie, who now pulled down their hoods. Absorbed as she had been by the passing scenery outside, Betty had failed to spot the Bray twins board the bus, with their friend, Jack. However, they had certainly spotted her.

The brothers had harboured a grudge against their neighbour ever since she'd stolen their guinea pigs, and made fools of their father and his cousin, Rowena. Being cut from the same cloth as Mr Bray, they were not brave enough to do anything directly to Betty, as they feared she'd put a curse or a spell on them. Instead, they had been waiting for a chance to do something anonymous and sneaky. Unfortunately for her, today they had been presented with the perfect opportunity.

Inside the woods, Betty heard the engine of the bus start up and pull away from the roadside. She lay amongst the vegetation, still too stunned to get her thoughts in order. What had just happened? Why had the boy done such a cruel thing?

As the late afternoon passed and evening set in, the light began to fade, and Betty was beginning to despair. She'd tried a number of times to get back up on to her feet, but the pain in her ankle was just too excruciating. All she could do was crawl out of the deep undergrowth, on her hands and knees. Leaning her bodyweight against the comforting thick trunk of an ash tree, she shut her eyes.

Tears began to stream down her cheeks, not because of the physical pain, but because she was angry with herself for being helpless, and for being duped by a child. She was even more upset at the prospect of the Greenwoods' animals going hungry. Whatever was she to do?

Chapter 21

The Missing Pomeranian

BACK at Bowood, Piggy Mama was puzzled. Something was not right. There had been no sign of Madam Pom since early morning. She was not in the garden or the house. There was no loud snuffling, no noisy snoring, and no pompous pedigree imperiously trotting around her territory. It was most odd.

Skip was totally unaware. He was so used to Madam Pom's lazy days, where she did not move from her bed, that he had not noticed her absence. He was too busy frolicking in the garden, chasing squirrels and sniffing around the flower beds.

Hazel, Alfie and Little Rufus were jubilant. Ha, ha – no stuck-up pooch to spoil things!

They would enjoy a day of freedom, without Madam looking down her nose at them, disapproving of their fun and making caustic comments. They each celebrated the pleasing news by settling down contentedly in their sweet meadow hay, and tucking into some tasty left-over chunks of carrot.

Mama went to raise the alarm with Skip, but Hazel, Alfie and Little Rufus maintained their lack of concern. Why should they care about that bothersome dog? When did she ever say anything nice to them?

Apparently, they were vastly inferior to her, so why should they care if she was gone? They each carried on nibbling their crunchy sweet carrot. It tasted so good... or at least it had a few minutes ago. Now, it began to lose its flavour. Hazel swallowed hard to try and lose the small niggling feeling which was gnawing away at the pit of her stomach.

Huh, what difference did it make to her if the Pom never came back? Her chewing became more laboured, and somehow the carrot pieces became less sweet and juicy. They were beginning to taste of absolutely nothing, and became harder and harder to swallow.

Hazel found herself thinking back to the bad old days of Oakfield Lane, when the piggies found themselves abandoned and unloved. It brought back a flood of emotion. What if Madam was lost? What if she had been stolen? What if she was wandering the streets, far from home? She shivered.

She looked across at Alfie and Little Rufus. Their faces told a similar story. Alfie stared back at her with an uncomfortable look in his eyes. His carrot sat in front of him, unfinished. He too had the funniest feeling in his stomach: it was getting tighter and tighter. Oh no, he was having... he didn't even like to consider it... feelings!

Hazel, Alfie and Little Rufus stared miserably at one another, the truth slowly dawning on them – they did actually care about Madam Pom, whether they liked it or not.

Little Rufus tried blinking hard in the hope that the horrid unwanted sensation would go away, but it didn't. He shut his eyes to block it out completely, but all he could see was a shivering Pomeranian, all alone in the world, cold and afraid.

"What should we do, Mama?" asked Hazel.

"We must wait for Betty to get here," replied Mama. "She'll notice that Madam's missing and do something."

That was the best plan they could come up with. At that moment, it seemed the only option.

That, however, was until darkness was ready to fall, and there had been no sign of Betty arriving. How very strange. It was well past supper time. Betty would never let them down.

It was time to speak with the sprites.

Down to the end of the garden, the piggies went, in the half-light of the evening. Hazel led the way, as always, and the others: Mama, Alfie, Little Rufus and Skip, followed in her wake.

Down, down, down, they walked, over the stepping-stones, past the birdbath and the sundial, past the flowers and the shrubs, right down to the silver birch tree and the ring of white marble statuettes at its feet.

"Merriel?" called Hazel softly.

She and the others watched, fascinated as always, by the sight of the pale figures transforming on either side of the Moon Queen's statue. A slight glow appeared around their edges, followed by a slight

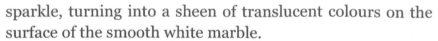

sparkle, turning into a sheen of translucent colours on the surface of the smooth white marble.

Within moments, the four figures of Merriel, Godfrig, Fion and Oro had regained their full colour and movement to appear before them.

"We desperately need your help..." began Hazel.

After the full story had been explained, the four sprites looked thoughtful.

"We will look into this matter and get back to you," Merriel assured them gently. Each at the same time, their figures transformed once more, but this time into four orbs of light.

The orbs, each of slightly different colour, sparkled and glowed in the dim evening air, before disappearing from sight.

In time, as Hazel and the others kept anxious watch, the orbs returned and formed back into the familiar sprites of Earth, Air, Water and Fire. It was Godfrig who spoke this time.

"We have consulted with our fellow sprites of Earth and Air, Little Ones. It has taken some time, but we have received word that a human and a dog are both in the woods of Lundy."

The animals gasped in unison. The woods! Both of them?

Even Hazel was stunned into silence at this point, and thoroughly stuck for what to say next. The woods were so far away, and it was nearly dark. How had Betty and Madam both ended up there? What could they do about it with no humans around?

"We can assist you," said Godfrig. "If you have the courage, we could escort you to the woods and protect you along the way." He stopped and added gently, "But it is a long way for little ones, like yourselves." It was clear what he was thinking. Guinea pigs did have rather short legs.

Hazel thought hard, and then announced, "I'm willing to go alone, if Skip will carry me on his back."

Skip, loyal and eager as always, instantly agreed. Mama was horrified by the whole idea and protested loudly. Alfie insisted that he should go along for added support, whilst Little Rufus clamoured to be included too. All spoke at once and chaos reigned.

It took Godfrig to raise his muscular hand and call over their heads, to calm the situation. "It is quite some way to the woods, and not an easy journey in the dark. It will be strain enough on our friend, Skip, to carry just one of you. We all know that one should be Hazel."

There was no more argument to be had, and no time to lose. Merriel and Oro gently shepherded Alfie, Mama and Little Rufus, back up the garden, and into the house.

Meanwhile, by the light of Fion's lantern, Godfrig helped Hazel and Skip to prepare for the journey, working quickly before nerves had time to set in. They faced a long night ahead.

Chapter 22
The Fields by Moonlight

THE gap in the hedge, used by Madam Pom to escape, had now been discovered, and was about to come in handy. Hazel was able to pop through the same way, and Skip squeezed through after her. They crossed the orchard, on the other side, and found their way through the five bar gate, into the wildflower meadow. Skip now lay on his front, enabling Hazel to climb up onto his back. Godfrig placed a thick twist of vine around his neck, and around the back of Hazel, for support.

Thankfully, the sky was clear and the Moon quite bright, as Hazel and Skip began their long journey, led by Godfrig. Fion further assisted by lighting the way with her lantern. By now, they had been joined by Oro flying alongside, next to the floating orb of Merriel.

The journey through the meadow was not unpleasant. The grasses, though getting higher, had not yet reached the height of Skip, allowing Hazel to take in the scenery around her. It could never match the beauty of the day. The green of the grasses was still visible, but the fading light had stolen the vibrant yellows of the cowslips and the buttercups, making their colours hard to distinguish from the white oxeye daisies. The poppies too had lost their brilliant reds, as had the clover and the sorrel. As if to make amends, the honeysuckle blooms, in the nearby hedges, offered up their sweet perfume, and a welcome breeze cooled the air.

It was eerily quiet. Those creatures normally seen out at night: the owls, the foxes, the badgers, the weasels and the stoats were laying low, wary of the light from Fion's lantern. Only occasional moths fluttered close by, drawn to the glow.

Little else disturbed the wildflowers and grasses, except the gentle breeze rustling the stalks and stems.

After some time, the meadows gave way to the wheat fields of Farmer Lewis. Enterprising foxes and rabbits had burrowed their way under gates, and through the hedges, leaving convenient pathways for Skip and Hazel to squeeze through.

As they made their way between the stalks of wheat, Hazel became increasingly nervous. They were now far from home, and the night was fast fading to full darkness.

The country folk of Brierley Bramble had always lived by superstitions. Many a cottage in the village still followed the ancient tradition of attaching horseshoes over their backdoors to ward off misfortune and evil spirits. According to Grama Lizzy, those foolish enough to venture out past nightfall were often warned, "Carry two crossed sticks of mountain ash for protection, as the dark holds many terrors."

Right now, the old folk tales, passed down through Grama Lizzy, were all Hazel could think of. Despite the reassuring presence of the four sprites, she could not forget what she'd heard of the perils that lay in wait for unsuspecting travellers – tales of evil spirits summoned by black magic; of hell-hounds with enormous jaws of piercing teeth; of ugly hairy boggarts, and bogles, and ghastly hobgoblins; of pale ghostly figures of wronged human maidens, seeking revenge upon untrue lovers...

Hazel had to bury her face deep into Skip's thick fur to stop herself from wheeking out loud. She clung on tightly and forced herself to concentrate on not falling from his back, as they began the uphill climb towards the woods. From Skip's breathing, she could sense his fear too.

Closer and closer they drew, until finally they approached the start of the trees. Hazel's heart sank as she spotted the unmistakable branches of a blackthorn tree – the tree of witchcraft and black magic. Its huge sharp thorns were enough to strike fear into any heart.

As if this was not bad enough, below its branches, a pair of large black ravens were playing tug of war with a long stick. Hazel's mind raced. According to the tales, these creatures were birds of death and ill omens, indeed the reincarnation of evil souls. Could her nerves take much more?

The two ravens stopped as Hazel, Skip and the sprites drew near. They flew up to perch on a branch of the blackthorn tree, eyeing them from above, with obvious curiosity.

Eventually, one of them called down, "Why hello, Oro, what an interesting set of friends you have with you!" The other raven croaked gleefully, clearly enjoying the joke.

Oro, the air sprite, looked calmly back up at them, "Hello Hubin. Hello Corby. Glad to see you haven't lost your sense of humour."

At this, the first raven fluttered down from the tree to stand before them. It was much larger close up, bigger than a crow or a rook, and quite alarming to one small guinea pig. Skip wasn't too keen either. The raven held its head to one side, puzzled by the sight in front of it: a guinea pig astride a small orange dog, accompanied by three sprites and an orb.

Despite her fear, Hazel could not help admiring the beauty of the bird. By the light of Fion's lantern, Hubin's feathers were shiny and sleek, his eyes resembling small black beads.

"Hubin," said Godfrig, "have you seen any creatures in the woods this evening, who don't belong, like a human or a dog?"

"Here after dark?" replied Hubin. "They would have to be foolish!"

"Indeed," called Corby, from the tree, "especially with the mood here in the woods tonight."

"Whatever do you mean?" asked Godfrig.

Hubin merely flapped his wings and began to fly away. "You'll soon see for yourself!" he croaked down at them. With that, he and the other raven flew away.

Puzzled, the animals and sprites continued their journey, taking their first steps into the wood itself. Soon, they gained some sense of what the ravens had meant. A feeling of heaviness filled the air, and weighed each of them down with an intense misery.

"Something's not right," said Godfrig. As an earth sprite, the woods were close to his heart. Many of his kind lived there, amongst the trees, stones and vegetation.

As the party of animals and sprites travelled further into the woods, Hazel was unnerved to see a myriad of tiny lights, like many luminous insects, appearing on the leaves and branches. They were joined by more on each stalk and stem of vegetation.

Godfrig turned to Skip and Hazel, "We must leave you for a short time. Stay here. We will return."

"Don't worry – you will be quite safe," added Merriel, kindly.

With that, the sprites each took orb form and floated up into the air above the heads of the dog and the guinea pig.

The bright sparkling orbs made a colourful display in the darkness of the night. As they hung in mid-air, the tiny lights lifted from the trees, stalks and stems, and surrounded them, like many moths floating around a flame.

Against the dark leaves and branches, the small lights had seemed bright, but in comparison with the orbs, they now appeared rather grey and subdued. As Hazel and Skip watched, the orbs slowly lost their sparkle and brightness, taking on the dull tones of the smaller lights.

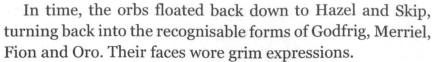

In time, the orbs floated back down to Hazel and Skip, turning back into the recognisable forms of Godfrig, Merriel, Fion and Oro. Their faces wore grim expressions.

Godfrig's eyes looked full of pain as he announced, "We have spoken with the sprites of the wood. Something dreadful has happened." His voice was soft, low and serious. "We need to go and speak with The Sage."

Chapter 23

The Sage

NEITHER Hazel nor Skip felt able to ask for any further explanation. They merely followed quietly, as Godfrig led the way, with Oro flying alongside, their path now lit again by Fion's lantern and the low light of Merriel's orb.

The party travelled on through the trees, each lost in their own thoughts. The sprites had taken on the sorrow of the woods. Whilst Hazel and Skip knew not the cause, they too had absorbed the low feelings, and felt no urge to speak. Yet their minds were full of questions. What was the cause of the grief? And who was 'The Sage'?

Further and further they travelled, until a thicket of beech trees came into sight. Here, Godfrig stopped. "Hazel, Skip," he said, "We are now approaching the ancient part of the wood. This has remained undisturbed by Man for many generations. It is a most special place."

The look on Godfrig's sad face had softened. Fion and Oro seemed to brighten too.

The floor of the wood now began to change. As the party travelled on, and the canopy of the beech trees was left behind, a carpet of bluebells offered up a delicate scent. Wood anemones and cowslips weaved alongside the wild garlic, leading the way to a clearing between the trees.

Lit by the moon, a magnificent oak tree stood in its centre. Its immense trunk was wider than two grown men with arms outstretched. Its thick sturdy branches towered up to the sky, crowned by lobed green leaves. Hazel and Skip both drew in their breath, sensing they were in the presence of greatness. This was indeed the King of the Forest, ruler of the trees, resplendent in this ancient part of the wood.

The oak had an aura of calm nobility, of wisdom and knowledge accumulated over centuries. The gnarled bark of the regal tree showed its age. Deep wrinkles and cracks lined its rugged surface, while lichens and mosses formed in and around the grooves. Here and there, gaps appeared in its mighty form, where woodpeckers and squirrels had found sanctuary and made it their home.

As the animals and sprites drew close, Godfrig called a halt. "This," he explained, "is where The Sage lives. His home is the hollow of the tree, deep within."

Godfrig paused. His gaze was resting on a mass of slim stems, with pointed leaves, clustered around the base of the oak tree, and extending outwards for quite some way.

"That, my friends, is dog's mercury," said Godfrig. "Hazel and Skip, you may not want to go any further."

Not much explanation was required, as a faint but decidedly unpleasant odour began to reach the sensitive noses of guinea pig and dog.

"When The Sage is not in a good mood, he encourages it to grow," said Godfrig. "It keeps everyone at a distance. The plant is poisonous – you won't want to be up to your noses in it."

After some thought, Godfrig announced, "Merriel, Fion, Oro – keep these two company whilst I go and seek a friend of mine."

Godfrig disappeared, and returned, in a short time, with a small dark creature beside him. It was a mole. "This is Neavus," he announced, "and he is going to help us. He will dig a tunnel beneath the plants to allow a different route up into the oak. Sorry, Skip, but because of your size, it will have to be Hazel alone from here."

Skip, amiable as ever, understood and lay down to allow Hazel to step from his back.

This left Hazel face to face with the mole. He was the oddest creature she had ever laid eyes on. He had glossy silky black fur with a pink twitching nose, and tiny eyes. His front feet were more like large pink spades.

By the light of Fion's lantern, Hazel, Skip and the sprites watched as Neavus snuffled around the soil, before beginning to scratch at the surface. He snuffled around some more then truly set to work and began to put his heart into it. His front feet moved faster and faster as he got into the rhythm. Soon his head was disappearing below ground level, leaving his dark shiny back end as his only visible part.

Heaps of soil grew around the hole. The work rate of Neavus was incredible. It was as if he was swimming through the soil. Before long, he had completely disappeared from view. Godfrig, now carrying a spade, followed him in, to help with the work.

After a wait which seemed like an eternity, Godfrig reappeared. "So sorry, Hazel, Neavus is such a greedy little creature. He would not stop slurping up every worm we uncovered along the way."

Hazel swallowed hard. She wished he had taken even longer so she could put off the dreaded moment. Going underground, especially in the dark woods, did not appeal in any way. She took one last glance at Skip, who returned a sympathetic 'glad-it's not-me' look, and gave her ear a small lick.

Merriel and Oro stayed behind to keep Skip company, whilst Fion lit the way for Hazel to enter the deep tunnel, with Godfrig close behind her. Once inside, the surprisingly fresh rich smell of the soil surrounded her and actually calmed her nerves a little, helped in part by the coolness of the earth beneath her feet. She kept close to Fion's lantern, trying not to look at the eerie shadows cast by bits of roots, stones and twigs poking out of the earthen walls, and averting her eyes from the view of the journey ahead.

Time passed slowly, but finally the closeness of the tunnel gave way to a lighter feeling of open space. They had reached the inside of the oak tree. Fion was now able to put down her light, for the hollowed out space was lit by small lanterns, dotted around the walls.

Earth sprites, or gnomes as they are so often called, being that little bit closer to humans, frequently take on their customs and ways, and so it was with The Sage. The tree was

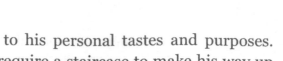

his home, fitted out to his personal tastes and purposes. Although he did not require a staircase to make his way up inside the higher levels of the tree, nor lights to see the way, he had them anyway, and chose to use them.

Once Hazel and the two nature sprites were clear of the tunnel, they paused on the roomy ground inside the oak tree. To Hazel's surprise, Godfrig now carried a stone flagon, with a large cork in the neck. It was just as before, when he summoned a spade out of nowhere, to dig the tunnel alongside Neavus.

"It's vintage oak leaf wine," Godfrig grinned, in answer to Hazel's puzzled look. "The Sage is not in the best of spirits at the moment, so this may help to soften his mood."

Hazel's heart began to race at the thought of meeting this most important gnome, especially if he was in a rather grumpy frame of mind. Would he welcome a visitor like her, not of his kind?

That question would soon be answered, as Godfrig led the way up the wooden staircase, which wound around the inside of the oak tree wall. Eventually, they came to a sturdy wooden door. Fortunately for Hazel, the staircase was quite wide, allowing her to walk up it fairly easily.

Without knocking, Godfrig turned the acorn handle, and pushed open the door. Hazel and Fion followed him into a spacious room. A large carved oak table filled the centre, surrounded by many skilfully crafted oak chairs. Wooden shelves, full of plates and goblets, lined the walls. Further lanterns lit the room, giving the space a warm glow.

A similar staircase led the way to the next floor. Again, Godfrig took the lead, but this time paused, as they reached another door. He politely knocked upon it.

A deep soft voice from within replied, "Enter, Godfrig, my good friend."

Godfrig pushed open the door and led Hazel and Fion into a smaller cosier room.

In a large plump armchair, with an oaken frame, sat The Sage. Like the tree he lived in, he was old and craggy, lined and wrinkled. He was in fact ageless, but his affinity with the tree he inhabited had made him take on its ancient appearance of rough bark. His white hair curled out from under his cap of green oak leaves, and fell below the level of his silky white beard. Large white eyebrows shaded a pair of soft brown eyes, in a kindly face. His red shirt, beneath a green waistcoat, was rolled up at the sleeves to reveal weathered nut-brown forearms.

One of these rested on the wooden table next to him, where there also sat a goblet and a plate. His other hand held an acorn stem pipe, from which wisps of smoke emerged.

Like the tree he loved, he had an unmistakable aura of calm wisdom, but also of sorrow. The brown eyes which turned to greet the visitors bore a troubled look.

"Welcome," he smiled gently. "Do take a seat each of you."

Godfrig and Fion each drew up a high-backed wooden chair to sit upon, whilst Hazel was offered a large plump cushion. She was then introduced to The Sage, who did not seem remotely fazed by the appearance of a guinea pig in his home.

His look of sorrow softened when Godfrig, his fellow earth sprite, presented him with the flagon of oak wine. "Do take a couple of goblets from the side there, for you and Fion, my good fellow," he said, "and join me in a drink." He glanced at Hazel and added, "There should be a bowl there too, which our new friend may find it easier to sup from."

He poured the oak wine. As Godfrig, Fion and The Sage raised their goblets, Hazel lapped a little from the bowl placed on a stool in front of her. The delicate green liquid had a refreshing slightly fruity taste, of understated sweetness. She drank a little more and settled down, feeling rather more relaxed than before.

"My Sage," said Godfrig quietly. "We heard the sad news from our friends in the wood – about the young oak trees."

"Ah, yes," nodded The Sage, his eyes clouding over once more. "One of them is now lost to us, and the others will not be far behind."

"Oh, my goodness," exclaimed Hazel, her tongue loosened by the oak wine, "Whatever has happened to them?"

Godfrig and Fion shot a startled glance at Hazel, a little taken aback by her direct question to The Sage, delivered without the usual deference he might expect. However, he merely smiled, appreciating her interest and concern.

"Why, Hazel, it is the usual story of Man's careless behaviour. Yet again, they have been spraying ghastly substances over the crops, on the town side of our woods. Although the aim is to kill what they see as nuisances and weeds, the wind carries those dreadful liquids to other places too. Three young oak trees, growing some distance from the woods, have been caught by them repeatedly, causing their tender leaves to twist and distort. Without their leaves, they can gather no energy. Their branches have begun to wilt over time and die. They are losing their battle to survive. Indeed, one of them has succumbed today."

The Sage's voice dropped to a whisper as he uttered the last sentence. "The other trees had been trying to support them through our underground networks, supplying as many nutrients as they could, but the best nutrition in the world cannot fight the terrible poisons they are receiving at the hands of Man."

He put his pipe to his mouth. He bowed his head, and fell silent. Hazel, Godfrig and Fion did the same, thinking over the solemn news, and sharing The Sage's grief.

After a few moments however, The Sage raised his head, breathed in deeply, and held out his goblet. "Come now, Godfrig, what can't be changed, must be tolerated for now. Refresh my cup, and those of our friends, and tell me what brings you to see me."

Godfrig explained the problem in full. The Sage listened attentively, expressing his genuine concern at the situation. At the end of Godfrig's account, The Sage left his chair and crossed over to the wall of the room. He lay one of his brown leathery old hands on the wood – the inner side of the ancient oak tree.

He closed his eyes and stood stone still, as if silently communicating. Indeed, the underground network of roots and fungi was speaking to him, reporting back from across the woods, with messages a human could never hear. Nature was working together as one.

His eyes opened once more, and The Sage looked at his guests. "My friends, Lucim the owl awaits you outside. She will assist you in your search. Put your faith in her – she has the knowledge you require."

With that, Godfrig, Fion and Hazel bade The Sage a fond farewell and found their way down the wooden staircases, into the tunnel and back out into the darkness of the woods, where Skip, Oro and Merriel waited.

As promised, Lucim the tawny owl was perched patiently on a stone, nearby.

There was just time for Hazel to be helped once more onto Skip's back, with the thick loop of twine for extra safety. Then, they were off – Lucim spread her wings and took to the air.

Merriel, Oro, Fion and Godfrig, took orb form to follow, illuminating the way with their sparkling light. Skip had to run after them as best he could, jumping over clumps of vegetation, and dodging low lying branches. Hazel clung on for dear life, glad of the practice she'd had with Blake, the heron.

The pace was quickening. Lucim was flying at ever increasing speed, and the chase through the trees was getting faster – so fast, that Skip failed to see the dead tree branch which took his feet from under him. Next thing Hazel knew, she was flying through the air, only to land on a soft pile of undergrowth.

As she picked herself up, and looked around for Skip, she was surprised to hear a noise – it was a cough, a human cough.

"Hello?" called a voice. Hazel gasped. That sounded like Betty.

At that moment, Skip snuffled his way back to her side, licking her in concern. "Skip!" Hazel exclaimed. "Did you hear that?"

"Hello?" called the voice again.

With no sign of Lucim or the sprites, the decision was taken to investigate this themselves. Skip lay down as quickly as he could to allow Hazel onto his back. As the voice sounded a third time, they set off in the direction from which it came.

Chapter 24

A Dark Shape in the Woods

MADAM Pom was cold and afraid. Her relief at finding sanctuary in the woods had faded when she had woken up alone, surrounded by darkness. The proud Pomeranian's ears lay flat, her tail drooping low. A sense of quiet desperation filled her body, as her stomach rumbled with hunger.

Much as she hated to admit it, she was now missing her home. She longed to be walking through the meadows once again with Billy and Skip, or lying by Mr Greenwood's feet, her head resting on one of his slippers. She ached to sit on Molly's lap once more, watching the television. She'd even welcome the sight of the annoying creatures from the outhouse.

For a second, she thought she was hallucinating. Her sensitive nose imagined it could smell the perfume of Betty, the nice kind lady who came to visit, the lady with the softest gentlest hands. Then, there came a cough from the other side of the bushes. Was that a human being?

Madam Pom leapt to her feet and followed the noise.

Betty was not afraid of the dark, but she was worried. How hungry would the animals at Bowood be by now? Would the Greenwoods ever forgive her?

She'd picked a few leaves of wood sorrel, growing just within reach, and now sat nibbling on the leaves. Their sharp refreshing taste provided a little comfort.

Betty was generally a calm person, but when a furry paw touched her arm, she let out a loud startled shriek. She laughed with relief when she realised it was a small Pomeranian dog – in fact, it was Madam Pom! How on earth...?

Hazel and Skip were doing their best, but their pursuit of the human voice was not going well. Each time they felt they had nearly reached it, it seemed to move further away. Now a loud shriek caught their attention, in a completely different direction. Skip changed course, and navigated their way once more through the undergrowth between the trees – not easy in the darkness of night, with little light to guide them. Like most animals, they could see in the dark, but there were so many obstacles in their path, ready to catch Skip's slim paws, that he had to concentrate doubly hard.

Skip was beginning to struggle – he was fast running out of energy. The situation was becoming hopeless. As he stopped to draw breath and regain his strength, he and Hazel heard the voice call, "Hello?" from the branches above them. This was swiftly followed by a cough from another tree, and a further "Hello?" from yet another.

As a strange rustling came from the undergrowth nearby, a rising sense of panic engulfed both animals. This was clearly *not* Betty.

Madam Pom snuggled close to Betty, and licked her hand, so grateful to see her. Betty hugged her close, equally glad of the company. She was beyond baffled by the sudden appearance of the little dog, but assumed she had escaped from the Bowood garden because she was hungry, and no one had been around to feed her. It caused a strong pang of guilt.

Yet, she did not have long to dwell on this, for, seemingly out of nowhere, a tawny owl suddenly appeared, and swooped down to sit right beside her, as if to say hello.

The rustling was getting closer. Hazel had slipped from Skip's back to huddle close beside him, hardly daring to breathe. Her mind was racing. Was it a bogle or a boggart, or a ghastly hell-hound with enormous piercing teeth? They both froze in terror as a black shape emerged from the undergrowth...

"Stop!" ordered a voice behind them.

It was Godfrig. Hazel wanted to weep with joy. He'd saved them!

The rustling had stopped, and the wood around them now lay deathly quiet.

"Come out and show yourselves!" Godfrig commanded.

The rustling resumed, and, to the absolute astonishment of Hazel and Skip, two black shapes emerged from the darkness.

It was Hubin and Corby, the ravens.

"Why am I not surprised by your behaviour?" asked Godfrig, sternly. "You two could have been such a help tonight, but instead you chose to make mischief."

Godfrig put a comforting arm around Skip and Hazel, and explained to the still-trembling animals, "Our friends here are masters of mimicry. They can imitate pretty much any sound they hear. They clearly decided to have some fun this evening."

"Well, Hubin and Corby," he continued, "I'll leave The Sage to deal with you pair. My job now is to sort out the mess you have helped to create."

Croaking loudly, the ravens both flapped their wings, rose up between the trees, and were gone.

"I'd like to say they'll learn their lesson, but I doubt it," said Godfrig. "Those two can never resist devilment."

As Hazel and Skip breathed a huge sigh of relief, Godfrig gave them some welcome news, "You'll be glad to know that Betty and Madam are both safe."

Hazel clapped her front paws together in joy, whilst Skip twirled around on the spot, and panted loudly, causing Godfrig to laugh heartily.

As they did so, the orbs of Merriel, Fion and Oro arrived to join them, turning swiftly back to sprite form. "Are you both okay?" asked Merriel in a concerned voice.

"Yes!" chorused Hazel and Skip.

"Good," she smiled, holding out her clam shell, full of cool clear water. She gently stroked the heads of both Hazel and Skip as they drank deeply. Fion, Oro and Godfrig joined in, playfully ruffling up their fur.

"Right," said Godfrig, eventually. "Now that you are refreshed, it's time to reunite you with Betty and Madam. Hazel, let me help you up onto Skip's back."

Fion lit the way with her lantern once more, as Hazel and Skip, tired but happy, followed in Godfrig's wake.

Sometime later, as she and Madam dozed under the tree, Betty was shocked to be abruptly woken by Skip nuzzling her hand. She was beyond speechless when Hazel then jumped up onto her lap too.

Madam totally forgot herself and leapt up to greet them both, barking like an excited puppy.

Once all the excitement had died down, Hazel snuggled closely into Betty's lap, where Skip and Madam Pom now slept either side. She longed to tell Betty how she and Skip had got there, but knew she had no way to do so.

She realised the sprites had long since disappeared from view, but suspected they were still around somewhere, ready to help if absolutely necessary. Hazel knew she had to come up with a plan for getting home, as Betty did not seem able to get up or walk.

She thought back to the time when she'd flown through the sky on the heron's back, and Skip had been that small orange shape in the field. Of course! The answer lay with the kind man who had helped that day.

"Skip," she whispered quietly. "You remember the man who rescued you on his bike?"

"Yes," replied Skip.

"Do you know where he lives?"

"Of course, I've been taken there a few times, on our walks."

Hazel did not need to explain any further. Skip immediately understood why she was asking. He had a good sense of direction, and would soon find his way to P.C. Frankie's cottage.

Betty had fallen asleep once more, so Skip was able to gently lift his head from her lap and stand up, ready to take his leave. Madam Pom raised her head and asked where he was going. "Hazel will explain," he said.

With that he was off, running through the woods, in the direction of Brierley Bramble. It took a while, but he eventually arrived on the quiet lane where the police officer's cottage was located. Moments later, Skip was in his front garden.

As it was the early hours of the morning, all human life was asleep. However, in the window of the cottage, Tabitha, the Frankies' cat, lay snoozing but alert, on the sill. Skip barked softly to catch her attention.

The cat opened one eye in surprise. She recognised Skip, and sat up to look at him. When he barked again, she leapt down from the windowsill, and within seconds, appeared through the cat flap of the front door.

Skip hurriedly explained the situation as best he could. Tabitha listened and then went back into the house. Skip could hear her yowling at the top of her voice, as if in terrible distress.

She had known what she was doing, for within a short space of time, a light went on upstairs. The cat yowled some more, and then slipped back out through the flap, waiting patiently.

The front door was opened, and P.C. Frankie's puzzled face appeared, a torch shining in his hand. "Tabitha, whatever is the matter?" he asked, yawning loudly, and wondering why Skip was there too.

Tabitha yowled again and began to run off down the street, accompanied by Skip.

The police officer was surprised at the unruly behaviour of his normally very sedate cat. She usually slept soundly all night, never leaving the house till morning.

"Tabitha!" he called loudly in astonishment.

The cat, however, was showing no signs of stopping. P.C. Frankie, still in his pyjamas, had no option but to grab his bike from the side of his cottage, throw his torch into the basket, and race after his errant moggy, pedalling furiously.

Skip led Tabitha as far along the road as he could

(enabling P.C. Frankie to follow) but finally reached the point where they would have to enter the woods. They waited for the policeman to catch up before they both slipped between the trees.

The poor Brierley Bramble officer had to leap from his bike, grab his torch, and follow as best he could. It was not easy to do so in slippers, but he did manage to keep up with Tabitha and Skip, who deliberately took their time, keeping only slightly ahead of him.

Eventually, the situation became clear. P.C. Frankie's torch picked up the sleeping figure of Betty, propped up under a tree, with her arms around Madam Pom.

The policeman was aghast. Luckily for him, he didn't notice the guinea pig huddled up on Betty's lap, beneath her cardigan. That really would have pushed him over the edge.

Madam Pom barked excitedly as she heard him approach, which woke Betty immediately. The broadest smile of relief spread across her face when she saw who it was.

"Why, Jim! However did you find me?"

She laughed in disbelief when she heard how it was Skip and Tabitha who had led him there, and assured her anxious friend that there was no need to be concerned about her; she was absolutely fine, apart from her ankle.

Instinctively, Betty had ensured that Hazel remained well hidden. How the guinea pig had reached her in the woods was impossible enough for her to deal with, never mind P.C. Frankie. So, to avoid any awkward questions from the police

officer, she invented some tale about taking the two dogs for a walk in the woods, and carelessly tripping over a log.

Once satisfied that Betty was okay, P.C. Frankie returned to his bicycle, and used his police radio, attached to the handlebar, to summon help.

Within minutes, a paramedic drew up in his car, and was shown to the spot where Betty sat. She was pleased to recognise him as young Neville Frost from the village.

After a thorough examination, Betty insisted that she was fine, and all that she needed was a lift to the Greenwoods' home, where she was staying. A sprained ankle did not need emergency treatment, she stated firmly. She'd soon get a garlic poultice on it, first thing in the morning.

Neville reluctantly agreed, and with the help of P.C. Frankie, got her into the back of his car, along with the two dogs (and one hidden guinea pig). He never thought to ask how Betty had walked the dogs without any leads.

With Betty taken care of, P.C. Frankie picked up his cat, and put her into the basket of his bicycle. She was soon returned home, and safely delivered into the arms of his puzzled wife. He then went upstairs to get dressed. He needed to check that Betty had been safely delivered too.

Upon arrival at Bowood, Betty produced the keys for Neville. He let her in, and guided her to a comfy chair in the kitchen, where he strapped her ankle up, and insisted that she rest it on a cushion. After making her a good strong cup of tea, he fed the two dogs and put some food in the hutch of the guinea pigs, in the outhouse. He left her sitting happily by the warm Aga, with the spare walking stick that she kept at Bowood, by her side.

Once he was gone, Betty pulled Hazel out from her pocket, kissed the top of her silky head, and sat her on her lap.

"Well, well, little piggy," she said softly. "If only you could talk..."

Chapter 25

Home Sweet Home

IN the weeks that followed the woodland adventure, a number of strange things happened.

In the town of Morecaston, a rather large billboard had appeared on the high street advertising:

'Best Breed dog food, the complete nutrition for our canine companions!'

Mr Greenwood spotted it, as he drove Molly home from a night at her friend's house, with Billy in the backseat. None of them could believe their eyes. The accompanying picture was a huge image of a grinning Pomeranian, in a gold tiara and a pink feather boa. It was the exact spitting image of Madam Pom. How could there be two of them in the world?

Close by, came the second surprise. *Morecaston's Premier Photographer's Studio,* a favourite of the locals for well over twenty years, was gone. A cheerful sign on the door proclaimed,

'Shut down. Owner retired!'

Filled with curiosity, Mr Greenwood pulled over to ask for an explanation from a window cleaner, who was busily soaping a nearby shop front.

"Ha, ha," came the reply. "She came in to money, did that

Doreen." He nodded over at the billboard. "She sold one of her pictures for a right princely sum. My mate saw her driving off in a nice new motor – soft top it was, and bright purple!"

They couldn't wait to get home and tell Betty, who was still recuperating at Bowood, at Mr Greenwood's absolute insistence.

She laughed heartily, and then offered some interesting news of her own. According to one of her neighbours from Oakfield Lane, the Brays had disappeared too.

There had been a peculiar incident. A power-cut had hit the Brays' house – no one else's, just theirs – leaving them sitting in the dark.

Investigations had revealed that their wires and cables had been completely chewed through by many, many small teeth.

Further trauma was to follow. They had woken up, the morning after, to find their garden strewn with hundreds, upon hundreds, of yellow feathers, in the trees, on the flowers, and across the lawn...

The upshot was, they had fled their home, leaving only a *for sale* sign behind.

Despite Betty's general good nature, she had allowed herself a little giggle of guilty pleasure at this surprising piece of news.

Madam Pom had been so nice to everyone, after the incident in the woods. She had not made one single haughty comment, nor one acidic criticism. There had been absolutely no eye-rolling or contemptuous sighs. It felt most odd, and lasted for a whole week, but no longer. She soon returned to normal after that.

The piggies didn't mind, nor did Skip. They were well used to her by now. They were just so grateful to be back at Bowood, and living their happy lives once more.

That night, a Full Moon heralded the return of The Moon Queen. The guinea pigs and the Pomeranians were summoned to a small celebration with herself and the four sprites.

Under the silver birch tree, by the light of Fion's torches, they talked over the events in the woods, and all that had happened since Her Majesty's last visit.

The animals were treated to a few refreshments, supplied by Godfrig: fresh flavoursome dandelion leaves for the piggies, and sweet crunchy carrots for the Poms, washed down with fresh cool water from the clam shells of Merriel.

Delicate scents of gardenias perfumed the night air, as Oro played cheerful tunes upon his reed pipe. The atmosphere was relaxed and cheerful as the sprites played games with the animals and danced around in the moonlight.

Eventually, it was time for the evening's entertainment to come to an end.

So, after paying their respects to The Moon Queen and her sprites, the guinea pigs and the Pomeranians headed off to bed, happy, content and ready for sleep.

Skip was soon breathing quietly on his soft comfy bed, whilst Madam Pom snored loudly on hers. Once settled down in the sweet meadow hay of their hutch, Piggy Mama, Alfie and Little Rufus were soon sound asleep.

Hazel was not.

She slipped quietly down the ramp below the hutch, squeezed out under the wire netting of the run, and crossed the floor to the hidden hole in the wall.

Emerging from behind the camellia bush, she wandered down to the lawn, and sat silently on the soft grass, enjoying

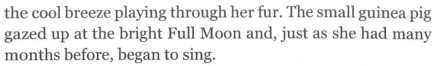

the cool breeze playing through her fur. The small guinea pig gazed up at the bright Full Moon and, just as she had many months before, began to sing.

As her last note floated away on the light wind, a few tiny drops of rain began to fall.

Hazel drew in a deep breath, closed her eyes, and pictured Piggy Papa in her mind. She thought over the life she once had, the life she had now, and wondered about the life still to come.

A new surge of happiness coursed through her veins. She awoke from her reverie, and rose up onto her back legs, surprised to find she could now move forward, just as easily on two, as she could on four.

She took one hesitant step forward, followed by another, and her confidence steadily grew. Her movements became quicker and smoother, higher and longer. She could now put her weight on one foot alone, so she did – first one, and then the other. In time, she found she could dance, and so she did – leaping, twirling, spinning and pirouetting.

As she capered on the lawn, a luminous form appeared in a corner of the garden. It was a silver white hare, with slim delicate limbs and tall slender ears. Its piercing silver blue eyes watched Hazel for a few long moments, then turned and melted away into the night.

The rain grew heavy. Time moved on. But the piggy did not care.

Hazel just carried on dancing in the rain.

Dear Reader

As I'm sure you know, guinea pigs are adorable little creatures, who make wonderful pets for children and adults alike. They are friendly, sociable and curious. They will 'talk' to you and return all the love you give them.

However, in homes across the world, many suffer miserable lives, as do neglected pets of all shapes and sizes. Guinea pigs (like rabbits) should not simply be stuck out in a hutch in the garden. They need protection from predators and extremes of temperature, and must have plenty of room to move.

Dogs too need exercise and company. So many people buy a dog and expect it to simply stay home all day – bored and lonely!

Let's spread the word and educate people on their responsibilities to the animals in our care. After all, we create and control their entire world. Their happiness depends on us.

Encourage others to do their research before buying any pet. Do they know what its needs are before they make the decision to buy? Do they have the time, ability and motivation to care for it properly? Guinea pigs have quite different needs from rabbits, and one breed of dog can differ considerably from another.

For excellent sources of information on piggies, see:

guineapigmagazine.com

theguineapigforum.co.uk

Peter Gurney: **calicavycollective.com**

For dogs, see the help and advice pages at:

dogstrust.org.uk

If you find a sick, injured or abandoned wild bird or animal:

helpwildlife.co.uk

Equivalent organisations can be found online across the world.

About the Author

In memory of all the piggies
who have shared my life over the years:
Sally, Titch, Pip, Duggie, McGuffy, Hazel, Ruby, Blossom
and Rosie,

and with love for our Poms:
Sasha & Lola.

J.P. Stringer lives in Derbyshire with her husband, three
children and two Pomeranian dogs.
Contact her on: **brierleybramble@gmail.com**

About the Illustrator

KIM FOWLER ILLUSTRATION
& fine art

Kim Fowler is a traditional style illustrator and artist who creates highly detailed drawings inspired by fairy tales, mythology, historical figures and the fluidity of the Art Nouveau period.

Her illustrations are heavily steeped in symbolism, and almost every element translates into the overall narrative of the piece.

Kim likes to create windows into an esoteric world and invites the viewer to get lost within the detail.

(f) /kimfowler.illustration

(ⓘ) kimfowlerillustration

(y) kimillustrate

(✉) kimfowlerillustration@live.com

www.kimfowlerillustration.co.uk

My Heartfelt Thanks To:

Jim: For your continued love and support, with everything, always, and for your sterling efforts in editing this book and smoothing out all the wrinkles.

Robb, Will & Eve: For all the happiness you bring, the second opinions you offer and the help you provide with all things technical.

Sarah, Ian, Isabel & Christopher: For bringing happiness, albeit long distance.

Hazel Douglas (and piggies: Alfie, Lizzy & Rufus): For being my cheerleader from the start, and for providing sound advice along the way. The story would never have got off the ground without you.

Kim Fowler: For your skilful, intelligent and witty artwork which brought this story to life on the page.

Adrian Doan Kim: For your glorious cover design and illustration.

Fiona Birney: For your perfect book design, formatting and typesetting.

Alison Byford of Guinea Pig Magazine: For playing a helpful part in all my guinea pig ventures over the years.

Kieran (K- Dogg) Walker: For your brilliant feedback and superb proofreading.

Sharon Hawkins: For your help and enthusiasm.